"Quick, you've got to get out of sight!"

Sam's voice was hard and impatient. "I just saw Denise's car, and if she finds out you've been here all night, we're both going to wish we'd never been born."

Annabel couldn't believe it. "Are you engaged to her?"

"I've asked her to marry me, yes."

Annabel knew the financial hold Denise's father had on Sam. She looked at him with uneasy eyes, and he stared back as if her silence said something more audible than words.

"All right, I'll give Charlie his job back! Now will you go upstairs until I can get Denise away from here?"

Annabel turned and ran. Sam believed she'd been stalling as some sort of blackmail, but that wasn't what had held her back. She had been overwhelmed by totally primitive jealousy!

CHARLOTTE LAMB began to write "because it was one job I could do without having to leave the children." Now writing is her profession. She has had more than forty Harlequin novels published since 1978. "I love to write," she explains, "and it comes very easily to me." Once she begins a story, the plot, the actions and personalities of her characters develop almost spontaneously. She and her family live in a beautiful old home on the Isle of Man, between England and Ireland. Charlotte spends eight hours a day working at her typewriter—and she enjoys every minute of it.

Books by Charlotte Lamb

These books may be available at your local bookseller.

Don't miss any of our special offers. Write to us at the following address for information on our newest releases.

Harlequin Reader Service
901 Fuhrmann Blvd., P.O. Box 1397, Buffalo, NY 14240
Canadian address: P.O. Box 2800, Postal Station A,
5170 Yonge St., Willowdale, Ont. M2N 6J3

CHARLOTTE LAMB

explosive meeting

Harlequin Books

TORONTO • NEW YORK • LONDON
AMSTERDAM • PARIS • SYDNEY • HAMBURG
STOCKHOLM • ATHENS • TOKYO • MILAN

Harlequin Presents first edition July 1986
ISBN 0-373-10898-2

Original hardcover edition published in 1985
by Mills & Boon Limited

CHAPTER ONE

'Do stand still, Charlie, or I'll strangle you!'

Annabel had to stand on tiptoe to reach the black tie which Charlie's fumbling had mangled. Evening dress suited him. A foot taller than herself, he was a broad-shouldered, rugged young man with thick, curly hair the colour of buttered corn. Most girls looked dreamily at him and they certainly would tonight—but those blue eyes of his were myopic in more senses than one. Charlie was too absorbed in his work to notice anything else, and if he forgot to put in his contact lenses he simply didn't see faces, anyway, just blurs.

'Do I have to wear this penguin suit?' he asked glumly and Annabel viciously pinched his ear.

'Yes, you do. It's a formal dance.'

Charlie rubbed his lobe, mildly aware of having felt something. Her small, slim fingers hardly registered on him.

'I still don't see why we have to go.'

'Everyone is going; this is the staff dance, remember. Don't be so annoying. And when you see Sam Jerrard you're to be very polite and friendly, don't just hang about looking sulky. Have you got your lenses in?'

'Yes,' he said a little too quickly and she peered suspiciously at him. She knew Charlie very well because he had been at school with her brothers— all five of them—and they had grown up together, although his closest friend among the Walsh boys had been Patrick, who was just over a year older than Annabel, and her favourite brother. She had spent most of her childhood running around the Norfolk broads with Charlie and Patrick; fishing and swimming and falling into the water.

'I hope you're telling me the truth,' she said with severity. Charlie hated wearing his contact lenses; he said they made his eyes water.

He reddened guiltily; he had never been very good at telling lies.

'Put them in!' Annabel ordered immediately and he fumbled for them in his jacket pocket, grimacing. She watched in satisfaction as he inserted the lenses. At least now he would be able to see Sam Jerrard if he got a chance to talk to the man. He wouldn't just blunder past him, or knock him over. Charlie had the grace of an elephant when he couldn't see where he was going.

He focused on her, his expression placatory. 'You look marvellous,' he flattered and she grinned at him.

'Thanks, but don't overdo it.' Annabel Walsh had been a bitter disappointment to her mother as it became clear that she was not going to grow up into a raving beauty.

Elaine Walsh had had five sons, one after another. Much as she loved them all, she had increasingly longed to have a daughter—one child, at least, who wouldn't come home covered in mud from playing football, who wouldn't get into fights or fall into the nearest water as the Walsh boys often did—unless, of course the nearest water happened to be a bath, in which case the boys had to be dragged to it, whining like rabid dogs.

When her sixth, and last, child was the girl she longed for, Elaine Walsh had been over the moon, convinced by the baby's wisps of pale hair and blue eyes that all her dreams had been answered, and that when she grew up the baby would be a gentle, feminine blonde with a soft voice and a heart as tender as Elaine's own.

'I'll call her Annabel,' she said and the assorted masculinity around the bed made incredulous, disgusted noises.

'Annabel . . . yuk, sounds like a cow,' said burly, eight-year-old Joe.

Mr Walsh put out his index finger to touch the baby's cheek and Annabel's pink starfish hand grabbed and held on. Delighted, Philip Walsh smiled at his wife. 'With a grip like that you'd do better to call her Hercules.' Annabel turned her head and tried to eat his finger, bubbling with greed, and her brothers seethed around the bed, laughing and encouraging her, until the midwife drove them all out and left Elaine peacefully lying with her daughter, gazing at the innocent petal-soft face with eyes full of vain imagination.

If she had but known it she was too late—the Walsh men had already decided to appropriate Annabel and re-mould her in their image. Elaine Walsh hadn't expected Annabel's hair to turn red, a wild flame red which only had a touch of gold in strong sunlight. Nor had she expected Annabel's eyes to turn green, the bright, dangerous green of a cat's, with around the slit-like black pupil fine rays of yellow which glowed when she was in a temper. This was a frequent occurrence, which distressed Elaine Walsh but delighted the males of the family so that they shrieked with laughter when Annabel toddled after them, beating them with her small fists, red-faced with fury over some injury.

Years of fighting with her brothers developed Annabel's muscles. She was what her mother liked to call petite, five foot three in her bare feet, but her brothers taught her to box and swim, sail and fish, play football and cricket and run like the wind. At twenty-three she had a slim, boyish figure and was usually seen in jeans and shirts, except at work, when she wore the usual uniform of a lab technician—a white overall. Even in her choice of a job she had disappointed her mother—Elaine couldn't understand Annabel's passion for science fiction and, later, chemistry. But the need to be patient and keep calm which her job imposed had at least controlled Annabel's hot temper and curbed her impulsive urge to assert herself, natural enough in a girl growing up in a house full of pushy men but hardly, Elaine felt, likely to attract a husband. When she was unwise enough to say as much to Annabel she wished she had held her tongue.

Annabel had laughed so much that her brothers had run to find out what was so funny, and they had all then laughed, too.

'Who'd marry Annie?' Joe had asked, hooting.

Annabel sobered at that, glaring. 'What?'

Joe was by then a broad-shouldered, rugger-playing young man of twenty-six, but he had learnt to be wary of his sister when she looked like that. He had backed off, suppressing his grin.

'If I wanted to get married I bet I could,' Annabel had said, looking at them all in turn, daring them to contradict her. 'But after living with you lot for eighteen years, the last thing I'd ever do is get married. I'm not crazy enough for that.'

'You're crazy enough for anything,' Patrick said and then the boys all fled while Elaine sat sighing as she mended yet another torn football jersey.

In one sense, though, Annabel had been right—when she took the trouble to dress like a girl, coaxed her thick hair into sleek obedience and put on a little make-up, she could make a very different impression, and tonight she was wearing quite a sophisticated evening gown, her smooth shoulders bare and the low cut of the neckline suddenly making Charlie aware that, as well as muscles in her arms and slim, tanned legs, Annabel had been developing high, firm breasts. He had never really noticed them before, and his eyes rounded, staring.

'Annabel, that dress is very . . .' Rather pink, he looked for the right word to describe how the dress made her look, but Annabel wasn't listening, she was thinking on quite a different track.

'You can dance, can't you?' she asked, suddenly agitated.

Charlie shuffled his feet. 'I've been to the odd disco at college but I'm not keen on dancing.'

'Charlie, this is a formal dance,' Annabel said. 'They'll play a different sort of music—waltzes, foxtrots, that sort of thing.'

He looked disgusted. 'Old time dancing, you mean?'

They both worked for the Jerrard Foundation Laboratories, which was the largest firm in the

small Norfolk country town where they lived.
Tonight was the annual staff dance, to which
everyone who worked at Jerrard's was expected to
go. It was the one occasion on which his
employees could be certain of seeing Sam Jerrard,
who turned up every year to open the evening by
dancing with the oldest female employee, the tea-
lady, Mavis.

Mavis was fond of telling newcomers that in the
beginning, fifteen years ago, there had only been
Sam Jerrard, two young lab assistants and herself
in the firm. Mavis had cleaned, cooked a mid-day
meal, made tea and coffee and, as she put it, 'made
sure Sam didn't overwork'. The firm had grown
considerably since those days. Now there was a
self-service canteen which Mavis ran with the help
of another woman, but she still saw herself as the
linchpin of the whole operation, and she was one
of the few employees who called Mr Jerrard 'Sam'.

Charlie had joined the firm two years ago,
straight from university. He was passionately
absorbed in his own line of research on a new
fertiliser which he believed would revolutionise
agriculture in poor soil. Unfortunately, the
experiments he had to make were with volatile
chemicals, one of them nitrate, and Charlie tended
to get so engrossed that he became less careful
than he should have been. He had twice caused
explosions. The first was a minor affair, a few
broken test-tubes and bottles. But the second, a
few weeks ago, had destroyed an entire workbench
and blown out several windows.

Sam Jerrard had been violently angry. Waving a
handful of bills for the replacement of equipment

and windows and the re-painting of the walls and ceilings blackened during the explosion, he had told Charlie, 'We can't afford to employ a modern Guy Fawkes—if it happens again, you can find another job.'

Annabel hoped that, in the interval since, Sam Jerrard had had time to calm down and she was determined that Charlie should make a better impression on their boss when they met tonight.

'I'll have to teach you to waltz,' she decided ruefully now. 'It's very simple, you should pick it up quickly, but you'd better dance with me at first and don't ask anyone to dance until you're sure the band is playing a waltz.'

'Maybe I shouldn't dance at all?' Charlie said hopefully.

'Of course you must! Thank God you won't have to dance with Sam Jerrard, anyway,' Annabel said with relief.

Charlie looked horrified. 'Dance with . . . good heavens, Annabel.'

She took his hand and placed it on her waist firmly. 'Stop looking like a petrified rabbit, and listen. It's very simple to waltz.'

Her father wandered in, his pipe in his mouth, and watched them with amusement for several minutes as Charlie woodenly tried to follow her lead. Annabel's long skirts swirled around her, making him stumble, and Philip Walsh decided it was time to rescue Charlie. Coughing, he held up one wrist, tapping his watch at his daughter.

'Aren't you going to be late?'

She froze, letting the unhappy Charlie loose. 'Oh, no! It's gone eight—we should have been there by now.' She brushed a cheek against her father's in flight. 'Don't wait up—I'll be late, remember.'

Elaine Walsh came into the hall as Charlie closed his car door on Annabel's billowing skirts. She stood next to her husband, her face wistful. 'She looks lovely, doesn't she? But black ... why couldn't she have picked out a white dress? We saw such a pretty one, with ruched chiffon and ...'

Philip put an arm round her, grinning. 'Annabel isn't the chiffon type.'

Annabel had only seen Sam Jerrard from a distance on the few occasions when he had entered the laboratory where she worked. She had not gone to university because she knew that, after launching five boys into their chosen careers, which for the elder three had meant years of supporting them at university, her parents could not really afford the expense of paying her, too, an allowance to supplement a small grant. Her father had never given any hint that he couldn't afford it, but Annabel's green eyes were sharp and observant. Their home was comfortable and happy, but it was undeniably shabby, and her father's car was old, like his suits. Her mother had always made her own clothes, as well as Annabel's. Elaine Walsh ran up the curtains and chintz chair covers on her old electric sewing machine, too, but Annabel knew that her parents never had a holiday. They spent each summer weekend out in the country, near their home: Philip Walsh fishing while Elaine embroidered table cloths or napkins, or both of them out in the small boat in which all the Walsh children had learnt to sail. They enjoyed those summer days, but Annabel knew her mother had dreams of visiting exotic foreign places one day—Egypt or Greece or Morocco, places she only knew from travel brochures and books. So when Annabel had finished school she decided to get a job in the laboratories in Blackstone, her home town.

Her work was careful, precise and painstaking, and endlessly repetitive—a matter of repeating the same experiment over and over again, perhaps for weeks, to make quite certain that the original premise was unquestionable. Her family hadn't been sure she could do it; Annabel was famous for her impatience and hot temper. They prophesied a short employment with the Jerrard Foundation, but they had been proved wrong. Once Annabel had got over the initial tedium of the first months she had begun to enjoy her job and she had been given far more responsibility as the years went by. She had been there for five years now; she was quite highly paid and was in charge of several other young technicians. All the same, at her level it was rare for her to see the man who had founded the laboratories. Sam Jerrard now operated largely in London and abroad, selling the projects which were originated and experimented with down in Norfolk, running the day-to-day business of managing the firm. Everyone said that he was a brilliant research chemist. The firm's fortunes had been based on Sam Jerrard's own first researches into plant growth and soil enrichment. He had started with a small personal capital, but today his company was quoted on the stock markets of the world at a constantly rising share price.

When Annabel and Charlie arrived at the Black Swan, once a medieval house of rest for pilgrims, attached to a monastery, but later becoming one of the coaching inns on the route from Norwich to London, they found the car park crammed with cars and the beautifully restored timbers throbbing with the beat of dance music. Charlie had to park further up the High Street; there was no room left in the car park. As they walked back to the entrance to the Black Swan, the spring wind blew Annabel's hair across her face and whisked her skirts upwards.

Breathlessly, she reminded Charlie, 'Try to meet Sam Jerrard, get him talking, make him see how vital your work is . . .'

'Yes, Annabel,' he meekly agreed, following her into the black-beamed, vaulted hall. 'But he isn't easy to talk to, you know. He's a pretty tough chap . . .' He broke off as a waiter brushed past him, almost sending him sprawling. Charlie's hand involuntarily jerked up to one eye. 'Oh, no, I've dropped a lens . . .'

Annabel peered at their feet. 'Don't just stand there, look for it!' She went down on her kees and began inspecting the parquet floor. The hall was empty, luckily, but she couldn't see the tell-tale glint of the lens anywhere, and, as she crawled forward, head bent, she heard the click of heels behind her and flung out an arm to bar the way. 'Please, don't walk just there . . .'

Her hand hit a man's leg; tautly muscled flesh under what a swift, sideways look told her was very expensive tailoring. At that second, Charlie gave a triumphant grunt. 'Got it!' He began to stand up. His knee caught Annabel in the back. She lurched forward just as the man beside her took a step. He tripped over her and they sprawled together on the floor. Inches away from icy grey eyes, Annabel froze, recognising her victim with a sinking heart. This was not how she had planned to meet Sam Jerrard.

'What are you doing there, Annabel?' Charlie asked in amazement, hauling her to her feet without a glance for the other man. By the time she had got her breath back and regained her composure, Sam Jerrard was on his feet too—but he was more observant than Charlie.

'I might have known,' he said grimly. 'Hallo, Draycott—I hope you haven't got anything explosive in your pockets.'

Charlie was brushing Annabel's skirt, muttering apologies to her. He looked up, aghast, mouth open in a bleat of horror. 'Oh . . . sir . . . I . . . good lord, I beg your pardon, I didn't see it was you.'

Annabel thoughtfully assessed the other man. At close quarters he was rather taller than she had imagined from a distance, or was that the effect of the closely fitting black evening suit? He did not have Charlie's rugger-playing build but that lean body looked formidable enough without such massive shoulders and obvious muscle. Charlie's strength was largely in his frame; his nature was lamb-like and sweet-tempered, and she had no problem getting him to do whatever she wanted. One brief inspection told her that it would not be so easy to lead Sam Jerrard by the nose. His face was hard-boned and unyielding.

'I suppose I'm lucky to have escaped without a few broken bones.' Sam Jerrard's mouth indented with angry humour. 'Try to enjoy the rest of the evening without smashing the place up, will you?' He briefly looked at Annabel, half turning, then looked again, his eyes narrowed.

'Have I seen you somewhere before?'

'I work for you.' She tried to sound pleasant but the words had an edge on them because she wasn't sure she had liked the way his gaze slid over her from her wind-blown red hair to her full, black satin skirts.

His brows lifted, fine and dark and incredulous, then he nodded and walked away with his private party hurrying after him. She stared after them, wondering who he had brought down this time. He usually had a girl with him, with whom he danced once he had performed all his duty dances with the older members of staff. He never danced with any of the younger girls on the staff, which naturally caused much heartburning among them, and each year they came along hoping that this time he would break with precedent. He wasn't married, which made him number one target for some of the girls but, although he didn't look it, Sam Jerrard was at least thirty-eight, so if he hadn't married by now Annabel suspected that he never would; he was probably a confirmed bachelor. Judging by the pretty girls he was seen around with he did very well without getting married; it would just queer his pitch.

'Two girls tonight,' she said to Charlie. 'I wonder which one he's with?'

'The thin one in blue is his secretary,' Charlie said, peering through one eye. 'Annabel, I've got to go to the cloakroom to put my lens back in . . . see you in five minutes?'

Annabel went into the powder room to run a brush over her wind-blown hair, listening to the gossip among three other girls, one of whom, more knowledgeable than either Charlie or herself, had already identified not only Sam Jerrard's secretary but the other girl, a pale blonde with eyes like round, blue glass.

'Denise Keiron,' Eve said, patting a black curl into place with a satisfied look at her reflection. 'Her father's the old fella with the white hair. He's a merchant banker.'

'How do you know?' asked a girl who worked in the same lab as Annabel.

'Oh, Jeanie, don't you read newspapers? James Keiron is one of our biggest shareholders—or, at least, his bank is, which comes to the same thing, I suppose.' Eve renewed the coral pink gloss on her mouth, silent for a moment, then looked at herself again. 'I'm not sure white's my colour; this dress looks too pale.'

'Is Sam dating this Denise whatsit?' Jeanie asked, wide-eyed.

'It was in the papers the other day . . .'

Annabel went out, leaving them to their gossip, and found Charlie hovering with one eye on the brightly lit ballroom, where people were already dancing to the small band, and one eye on the door of the ladies' cloakroom. He looked apprehensive, like a little boy afraid that his mother has lost him, but he cheered up as she appeared.

'Oh, there you are! Is this a waltz?'

'A quickstep—let's grab a table before they all go,' Annabel said, taking his arm and pushing him towards the door. They found a table in the furthest corner; most of the others were already taken. Sam Jerrard and his party had the largest, in the very centre of one wall, a clear space all around them as people carefully didn't obscure their view of the dance floor or the band. All the staff had come dressed in their best clothes, yet they couldn't match up to the gloss and glamour of the blonde girl in her ice-blue silk, her ears glinting with diamonds every time she turned her head. Her father leaned back smoking a cigar, one hand toying with a glass of brandy. He looked bored. Annabel saw him stifle a yawn.

'Hallo, can we sit with you?'

Charlie smiled amiably at the two girls from their own department. 'Of course you can, Jeanie. Hallo, Alison, you look very nice. You both do.'

The band had been having a short break but now they began again and Charlie looked urgently at Annabel. 'Is this . . .'

'Yes, come on,' she said, taking his hand. 'See you later,' she told the other girls and felt their eyes enviously following her, especially Alison's— she had never been able to hide her soft spot for Charlie, who was far too shy to take advantage of it.

'One, two, three, one, two, three and . . .' Charlie muttered, staring at his feet.

Over his shoulder she caught Sam Jerrard's quizzical stare; Annabel blocked it with a polite, automatic smile, then her small hand compelled Charlie to shift until they were further away from Sam Jerrard and his blonde.

'Don't count out loud and don't look down,' Annabel whispered in Charlie's ear.

He gave her a despairing look. 'Don't talk while I'm concentrating, Annie.'

'And try to swing me round more often, don't keep moving in a straight line,' she ordered.

He swung vigorously. Out of the corner of her eye she saw Sam Jerrard deftly remove his partner out of range of Charlie's jabbing elbow.

'I think,' Annabel said, 'we had better sit down.' She had visions of half the dancers mown down by Charlie's waltzing technique. Relieved, he dropped his hands and started to walk back to their table, leaving Annabel with the entrancing vision of Sam Jerrard's long-limbed body moving with lazy grace, his partner's body held like thistledown in his arm. The blonde looked dreamy, as well she might. I'd like to see her if she had to dance with Charlie, Annabel thought viciously. As Annabel had come here with Charlie she probably wouldn't get many invitations from the other men; they wouldn't want to tread on Charlie's toes. Those broad shoulders of his were deceptively threatening and had kept quite a few of the interested men in the company from approaching Annabel over the last year or two. Charlie had appropriated her by virtue of his long friendship with her brother and Annabel was too attached to him to hint that she'd like to see rather less of him and rather more of someone else. Actually, there wasn't anyone special she was interested in, so it really didn't matter that much anyway.

Several others had joined Alison and Jeanie at the table. Charlie sank into his chair with a sigh. 'Hot in here, isn't it?'

Annabel watched Sam Jerrard deliver the blonde to their table. A moment later he walked away towards the bar. 'Charlie,' Annabel said, 'get us some drinks, will you?'

'There's a waiter coming round,' he pointed out.

'He'll take ages—you go, there's a dear.' She kicked him under the table, her eyes flicking meaningfully towards Sam Jerrard's vanishing figure, and Charlie's eyes rounded as he got the point.

'Oh, yes, of course,' he said, getting up. 'What would you like, girls?'

He was gone for nearly half an hour. When he got back the table was covered with empty glasses, the waiter having reached them first, but Charlie's loaded tray of drinks was welcome, although the girls teased him a little about the length of time he had taken.

'Waltz,' Annabel pointed out, getting up a few moments later. She wanted to hear what Sam Jerrard had said. Charlie gloomily obeyed and this time she didn't complain about his moving lips and constant counting in between whispered question and answer. 'Did you talk to him?' she asked.

'One, two three, and . . . not really,' Charlie said.

'But you were standing next to him, I saw you,' she said.

'One, two three . . . yes, but everyone was talking. One, two, three.'

Annabel dug her fingers into his broad shoulder. 'Charlie! Didn't you manage to say anything to him?'

Charlie's hand clasped her waist tighter, yanking up her dress in the process. 'Of course. I said hallo, enjoying the dance, and he said yes and made some stupid joke and everybody laughed.'

Annabel frowned. 'Joke? What about?'

Charlie was brick red. 'He said he'd often wondered if I was as lethal outside the lab as I am in it and having seen me dance he knew I was. Bloody nerve. Stupid business, dancing, anyway.' He trod on her foot. 'Sorry. Where was I? Look, you made me forget where I was . . .'

They sat down but Annabel was no sooner in her chair than Sam Jerrard materialised at their table, smiling around the circle of faces.

'Good evening, I hope you're all having a good time?'

'Yes, thank you,' they chorused like well-trained parrots, the girls slightly squeaky with excitement, eyes bright with hope as those grey eyes inspected them. He looked like a pasha assessing his harem, Annabel thought bitterly, until his cool stare halted on her.

'Would you care to dance, Miss . . .?'

'Walsh,' she said, torn between refusing with a cold smile and accepting so that she could do for Charlie what Charlie had been unable to do for himself. Her hesitation was only brief; she stood up. 'Thank you,' she said and as they walked out on to the floor was aware of an assortment of eyes fixed on them; surprise, envy, fury among the milder emotions she felt vibrating among her fellow employees. Sam Jerrard was breaking his own tradition. He had asked one of the younger women to dance. It was just as well, she thought, that nobody from the laboratories had seen the incident in the hall when she and Sam Jerrard sprawled together on the floor. Only his party had been present and they weren't likely to spread the story. She hoped.

Dancing with Sam Jerrard was a very different experience to dancing with Charlie. His hand firmly gripped her waist, his long legs slid smoothly beside her own and she could abandon herself to the pleasure of the movement without worrying about where they would end up. Annabel had frequently had to lead Charlie when he tried to march straight from one side of the room to the other, in danger of knocking over any other dancers in his path. With Sam Jerrard, though, there was no question of anyone but him dictating where they moved.

'So you work in the laboratories?' he asked, as they swirled across the floor.

She turned her head eagerly. 'Yes, with Charlie Draycott. He's a brilliant chemist; I'm fascinated by his new project; it could . . .'

'Are you engaged to him?' he interrupted, watching her.

Her eyes widened. 'Engaged? No, of course not, but working with him every day I probably realise just how clever he is and . . .'

'You don't have to sell Draycott to me. He wouldn't be at Jerrards if I didn't know he was an original and inventive chemist.' He suddenly spun on his heel and she flowed with him, her hand tightening on his shoulder.

'You're a very good dancer,' she said involuntarily and he gave her a mocking, wry little smile.

'Thank you, you're very good yourself—but can we drop the subject of Draycott? I'm here to enjoy myself and I don't find him a happy topic. Is your hair naturally that colour?'

'Yes, it is!' she said indignantly, not sure she liked the way his eyes roved over her face and vivid, red hair.

'Incredible,' he murmured. 'I can't keep calling you Miss Walsh—what's your first name?'

'Annabel,' she said, absurdly self-conscious.

His eyes were half-closed, the gleam through his black lashes like the light of the early morning sun on cold water. 'Annabel?' He sounded dubious. 'How very improbable for a girl with hair that colour. Do people shorten it?'

'Charlie calls me Annie.'

His lids lifted; she was taken aback by the penetration of the full stare of those grey eyes. He was a most disconcerting man.

'Draycott again! He seems to be your chief topic of conversation. Is he as explosive in private as he is in the laboratory?'

Annabel blushed and was angry both with him and herself as she did so. Sam Jerrard observed her high colour with eyes like dry ice. 'He's a very muscular young man, but I hadn't had him down as a Don Juan—how old are you?'

The sudden change of subject threw her and she stammered. 'I . . . twenty-three. Why?'

'Idle curiosity,' he said as the music crashed to a finish. He released her and steered her back to her table, smiled around the uplifted faces again and left her to face the curiosity of her friends.

'What was it like, dancing with him?' Jeanie burst out.

'Is he a good dancer? What did he say?' asked Alison. 'Oh, he sends shivers down my spine!'

'So does Dracula,' Annabel snapped.

'When he looks at me in that cool, sexy way I just melt,' Alison breathed and then gave them all a demonstration, rolling her eyes and sighing before she swooned back against her seat and everyone laughed.

'You poor girl,' one of the guys from maintenance said, putting a hand on her forehead. 'I hope you'll survive.' He snatched his hand away. 'Ooh . . . red hot! What you need is a long, cool drink. Where's that waiter?'

Annabel glanced across the room at Sam Jerrard's table. He was raising a glass of champagne to his mouth. Over the brim of it his gaze skated over the dancers and touched her face for a second before moving away. The blonde girl was dancing with one of the senior chemists. Her father was apparently asleep, his eyes closed and his hands folded over his stomach. Sam Jerrard's secretary was just walking away from the table in the direction of the ladies' cloakroom. On impulse, Annabel got up and followed her. Sometimes a man's secretary could influence him, drop the right word in his ear at the right time. It wouldn't do Charlie any harm if Sam Jerrard's secretary was on his side;

she might soothe Mr Jerrard down if Charlie got into any more trouble.

The thin, dark girl was eyeing herself in the mirror when Annabel came in; their eyes met. 'Hallo,' said Annabel with a bright smile.

The other girl gave her a sour look, nodding. She renewed her rust-red lipstick while Annabel pretended to brush her hair and dust her nose with pale powder.

'We haven't met, have we?' Annabel said with determined cheerfulness. 'I'm Annabel Walsh, I work in . . .'

'I know,' said the other girl, her manner implying that she knew all she wanted to know about Annabel, but Annabel refused to be put off.

'What's your name?'

'Gwen Bridge.' The girl admitted it reluctantly, snapping shut her handbag.

'I like your dress,' Annabel said quickly, before she could walk out of the room. 'It's a lovely colour, what do they call that—aquamarine, isn't it?'

'Blue,' Gwen Bridge said flatly.

Annabel gave a rueful sigh. 'Am I being obvious?'

The other girl surveyed her with the faintest lightening of expression. 'I don't know, are you? Did you follow me in here to talk to me?'

'Afraid so,' confessed Annabel. 'You see, I tried to talk to Mr Jerrard but he wasn't very encouraging . . .'

'Wasn't he?' Gwen Bridge's eyes looked like little black buttons. There was a touch of scorn in her tone, but Annabel didn't give up that easily; she plunged on.

'You've heard of Charlie Draycott, I suppose? He . . .'

'Keeps blowing up the lab,' supplied Gwen Bridge in a different tone of voice, almost smiling. 'I've heard of him. Who hasn't? That last bang was almost heard in London. Sam went spare. It cost over five hundred pounds to replace the equipment alone.'

'I know,' Annabel sighed. 'Charlie's absent-minded, he always has been when he's absorbed. He's so wrapped up in what he's doing, he forgets everything else, but what he's working on is very volatile, you know. He can't always predict what reaction he'll get, but I'm quite certain he'll come up with the exact formula in the end. Mr Jerrard must know how these things happen—after all, he's a chemist himself. Surely he realises how brilliant Charlie is? It would be a tragedy for Jerrard's if they lost Charlie. He's sure to be snapped up by some other firm in no time.'

'And you don't want him to leave?' The other girl eyed her oddly, smiling. 'I see. When you started to talk, I got the wrong impression—I thought that it was Sam you were interested in.'

'Mr Jerrard?' Annabel stared at her incredulously. 'But I don't know him, I only met him for the first time tonight—you didn't seriously think I was interested in him?'

Gwen laughed, opening the door. 'Oh, but I did. It wouldn't be the first time a girl has tried to get to him through me.' She began to walk back into the ballroom and Annbel caught up with her. She was given a cynical little smile. 'Look,' Gwen said, 'you're wasting your time. I don't have any influence with Sam. He makes his own decisions and once he's made them he won't budge. If you're that worried about your young man, tell him to be more careful in future. It isn't just the cost of his experiments that worries Sam—it's the chance of somebody being badly injured one day. That could be very bad for the company; it might scare off some investors.'

Annabel crossly said, 'Mr Jerrard's reasons are always based on money—Charlie would hate to hurt anyone, too, you know—he never allows anyone to be present in the lab when he's working on the more volatile experiments. The only one at risk is always himself.'

They had almost reached the Jerrard table. She stopped talking as she realised that Sam Jerrard might be able to hear her—he was watching them as if he was listening, his mouth crooked with amusement.

'Having trouble, Gwen?' he asked in a slightly raised voice.

'Nothing I can't handle,' his secretary said. 'Goodbye, Miss Walsh.' She went over to sit down and Annabel walked away, her long black skirts rustling around her feet, hearing the laughter at the table behind her with fury. Were they laughing at her? She had a shrewd idea they were; she could feel eyes fixed on her back. It had been a mistake to talk to the secretary—Annabel wished she hadn't acted so impulsively. No doubt Gwen Bridge would repeat every word she had said to Sam Jerrard. Was that why they were laughing?

'When can we go home?' Charlie asked her mournfully when she sat down next to him. All the others were dancing. Charlie was building a log cabin from the matches in a free box he had found in the ashtray. Those large, spatulate fingers of his were amazingly delicate when he put his mind to it; she often wondered how he could, at one and the same time, be so clumsy too.

'Soon,' she promised, patting his hand. In a ballroom Charlie was as out of place as a bull in a china shop.

A fortnight later Annabel was working on some experiments with seedlings in the laboratory greenhouse when she heard a now familiar sound; an ear-splitting crash followed by the tinkle and clatter of breaking glass. Several panes in the greenhouse wall cracked across and the garden outside was strewn with flying glass splinters and decapitated spring flowers which had been sliced off during the spray of the explosion. Annabel stood rigid, briefly deafened. Her eyes closed. 'Oh, no.'

A moment later, she saw people running towards the lab where Charlie had been working alone. He had already staggered out into the cold sunlight, his hair standing on end. The whole wall of the laboratory had been blown in. Charlie's cheek was speckled with little dots of blood. So was his white coat. Annabel ran out to meet him.

'Are you hurt?' she gasped before she got there. Charlie shook his head. Annabel grabbed hold of his lapels and yelled, 'You idiot, you dangerous lunatic, you could have been killed!'

'I see what I did,' Charlie burst out, but he was not talking about the wrecked laboratory or the destruction of the experimental garden in which they stood. 'I made a mistake in the proportions, that's where I went wrong all along—it was really very simple, it wasn't the ingredients, it was ... Next time I'll ...'

'Next time?' Annabel fumed, shaking him violently. 'Next time? Charlie, can't you get it through your thick head? Once Sam Jerrard hears about this, there won't be any next time for you.'

Two hours later her prophecy came true. Sam Jerrard spoke crisply to Charlie on the phone, wasting few words. 'You're fired. Get out today and don't touch so much as a bunsen burner, ever again, in a laboratory belonging to me.'

Charlie joined Annabel in her car that evening, his face pale and dazed with shock. He didn't say a word as she drove him back to his home, but as she parked outside his house he looked round at her with unhappy eyes. 'I can't believe he means it. What will happen to my research? I can't take it with me; it was carried out at Jerrard's and belongs to him, but it's mine, all mine; it isn't fair. If he hands the project over to someone else they'll get all the credit for it—is that justice?'

'Talk to him,' she urged. 'Go up to London and see him, make him listen—of course it isn't just; you can't let him get away with it. If he makes you go, he must let you take your research work with you.'

'He won't,' Charlie said fiercely. 'And he won't see me, either. I can't talk to him, Annabel, he scares me rigid. I'm tongue-tied when I see him, the words won't come.'

She stared at him, biting her lower lip. 'Can't

you write to him, then? Put it all down on paper, surely you could do that?'

'I've never been much good with words. Physics or geometry—they're an open book, but words baffle me.' He shot her a furtive, pleading look. 'Annabel, couldn't you . . .?'

'Write a letter for you? I suppose I could, if you tell me what you want to say.'

'No,' Charlie interrupted, a childish look on his rugged face. 'Go to London and see him.'

Annabel sat up, jaw dropping. 'You're joking!'

'No, I mean it. You're so good with people— much better with them than I ever am. He'd listen to you.'

'You're crazy! I've tried talking to him about you, when I danced with him, and he refused point blank to listen. Why should he listen this time?'

'You're a girl,' Charlie said in a confused way. 'Guys like Sam Jerrard do listen to girls—he's likely to punch me on the nose if he sets eyes on me, but he'd be too polite to do that to you.'

'Well, that's something,' Annabel said drily.

'Oh, please go, Annabel!'

'I can't, you must see that!'

'You're my only hope,' he said desperately and her heart sank at the imploring eyes he turned on her.

'Charlie, don't say that!'

'Tell him I won't do any more experiments on a big scale until I'm a hundred per cent sure I've got the right proportions—there won't be any more explosions.' He paused, looking cunning. 'Or if there are, he can take the cost of repairs out of my salary. I can't say fairer than that, can I? You can persuade him, Annabel, I know you can.'

Through her teeth, Annabel said: 'Get out of the car, Charlie!'

'Promise you'll go.'

'Your mother is watching us through the front bedroom curtains—and heaven knows what she thinks we're doing.'

Even that didn't alarm him into leaving the car. 'Annabel, please!' he said, patting her shoulder like a clumsy but affectionate dog, gazing at her in that helpless way he had, and she closed her eyes to shut him out, sighing. Sam Jerrard hadn't listened to her at the dance. Why should he listen now? Annabel suddenly felt a surge of resentful irritation, remembering Sam Jerrard's mocking amusement. Who did he think he was, anyway? He'd brushed her off as if she was a fly buzzing round his head. She went pink and opened her eyes.

Charlie was watching her hopefully, head on one side. Annabel considered him with rueful eyes.

'I must be as crazy as you are . . .'

'You'll go?' Charlie broke into a delighted smile. 'Oh, thank you, Annabel—I know you'll make him listen.'

'You're dead right,' Annabel said with a high colour. 'This time Sam Jerrard is going to listen to me if I have to knock him down and sit on him.'

CHAPTER TWO

ANNABEL decided not to tell her parents why she wanted to go to London for the weekend. Her brother Andrew was getting married in a few weeks and she had been meaning to buy a new outfit for the occasion, so she told her mother that she was going to town to do some shopping, and then had a dicey moment when Mrs Walsh debated whether or not to go with her.

'I need some shoes and a hat; there's so much more choice in London.' Her mother pulled at one grey curl and began chewing it in a thoughtful way. 'I think I'll come with you, we could stay with Joe and Sandra. They keep inviting us and we never find time to go all that way.'

Annabel's eyes flickered and she opened her mouth to confess her true reason for deciding to go to London, but fortunately at that moment Mrs Walsh gave a groan.

'Oh, I'd forgotten! I can't come; the church bazaar's this Saturday and I'm doing the teas. I'm sorry, Annabel. Look, why not go next week? I don't think I'm doing anything then.'

Annabel said that she wanted to go this weekend to catch the last night of a play she had planned to see for months, and her mother accepted that with a rueful shrug. All the same, Annabel was relieved to be getting on the train that Friday morning, alone and without her parents knowing what she was up to. They would try to talk her out of it if they knew.

The Jerrard Foundation had one floor of a modern office block in Mayfair, within walking distance of Bond Street. Annabel found the place easily enough that Friday morning, walking through the jostling crowds on her way from the underground station, constantly fighting a weak desire to back out of the whole idea. She half hoped she would get lost or that Tessam Street did not exist, but she found herself in it before long and a few moments later was standing outside a double plate-glass door, which bore the gold lettering and company logo: Jerrard Foundation Laboratories, with a few wavy ears of golden corn. Annabel knew that one of Sam Jerrard's first research lines had been into pest control among cereals.

She gazed through the glass door at the spacious lobby. A girl in a dark dress was typing at a desk opposite Annabel. She kept breaking off her work to answer the phone on a small switchboard, deftly connecting callers to the office they were calling.

Out of an inner door walked Sam Jerrard's secretary to drop a pile of envelopes on the receptionist's desk. As she turned to move away, Gwen Bridge caught sight of Annabel lurking outside and halted. Her mouth twisted wryly.

Annabel pushed open the door and walked towards her. 'Hallo.'

'I can guess why you're here, but you're wasting your breath. Take my advice, go home and tell your young man to take up something less dangerous.' Gwen Bridge looked even more capable and calm here, in her own environment, than she had at a dance at the Black Swan. Her white blouse and pleated grey skirt, although so simple, had obviously been expensive and suited her much better than the dress she had worn at the dance.

'Can't I see Mr Jerrard, just for a few moments?' Annabel pleaded and was given a sardonic look.

'He won't listen. He just talked to the insurance company—they'll pay this time but before they renew the cover at the end of this year they'll demand that your young man goes. So even if Sam was prepared to forgive and forget his hands are tied.'

Annabel sat down on a chair beside and receptionist's desk. 'I'll wait, anyway. All I want is five minutes of his time. That isn't too much to ask, is it?'

Gwen stood, staring at her, then turned and went back into the inner office, closing the door behind her. The receptionist had been listening, open-mouthed. She gave Annabel a curious smile.

'Like some coffee? I was just going to make some.'

'Thanks, I'd love some. I like mine black with no sugar.'

The girl vanished and came back with two paper cups of coffee. She handed one to Annabel and sat down behind her desk with the other.

'That was quick,' Annabel said, inhaling the scent of the coffee with faint disappointment. It smelled of steam and little else.

'We've got a machine.' The receptionist put an

elbow on the desk and leaned towards her. 'Do you work down in Norfolk? You and Miss Bridge were talking about the latest explosion, weren't you? Mr Jerrard was furious, he really hit the roof.'

Annabel gave her a weak smile and sipped, suppressing a grimace. The door opened behind the receptionist and Gwen came out again. The receptionist hurriedly began typing.

'I'm sorry,' Gwen said with a flat sympathy. 'He won't see you. I told you he wouldn't.'

Annabel settled herself firmly on the chair, her expression mulish. 'I'll wait.'

'Then you'll wait for ever,' Gwen told her with sudden impatience. 'He's in a meeting which will go on all morning, and then he's going out to lunch. Be sensible, go home.' She turned and walked back into her inner sanctum, but Annabel stayed where she was under the curious eyes of the receptionist. She had promised Charlie she would save his job if she could, and she wasn't giving up that easily.

Two hours later, she was still sitting there. She was alone by then, and intensely bored, having read her way through a small pile of magazines the receptionist had found her. The other girl had just gone to lunch, handing her switchboard over to Gwen, who came out from her own office whenever the phone rang, but pointedly ignored Annabel.

At a quarter past one some men came out of the inner office, taking cheerfully. They glanced at Annabel and smiled and she smiled back, wondering when Sam Jarrard would be leaving.

Five minutes later the door opened again and she jerked to attention as a familiar lean, dark-suited figure walked towards her.

Sam Jerrard stopped, eyeing her without a smile. 'Didn't Gwen tell you that I wouldn't see you?'

Her chin lifted, deceptively rounded, immovably obstinate. 'I've got to talk to you. I'm not going until I have.'

'You're wasting your time—nothing on this earth would make me change my mind about that crazy man. Draycott's too dangerous.'

'I realise you're angry . . .'

'Oh, you realise that, do you? I was beginning to think you were almost as much a lunatic as your boyfriend.'

The sarcasm made her flush but she stuck to her guns. 'You have every right to be furious,' she began and he laughed harshly.

'Thanks. That makes me feel much better.' He looked at his watch then back at her uplifted, serious face. 'Look, Miss Walsh, this discussion won't get either of us anywhere. I gave Draycott an ultimatum a few weeks ago but it obviously didn't sink in. The man is a menace and I've had enough of him. I'm sorry you've come all this way for nothing, but I have other things on my mind. I'm late for an appointment as it is—I'm afraid I can't spare you any more time.'

She began to get up, dropping her handbag, but she was too late—Sam Jerrard was already striding out of the swing doors and by the time she had pulled herself together to follow him, he had disappeared. All she heard was the whine of the lift descending. For a second she almost followed him down the stairs, but it was six flights to the street and she would never catch up with him. With a sinking heart, she turned back into the lobby and found Gwen Bridge watching her.

'I won't say I told you so, but I did. Give up and go home—if your young man is as brilliant as you seem to think, he'll get another job and maybe he'll be working on something that won't blow up on him.'

Annabel wavered for a second, then remembered Charlie's desperate face and stiffened her resolve. 'I'm staying here,' she insisted and Gwen impatiently grimaced.

The receptionist came hurrying back from lunch at that minute, her face flushed by a tussle with the spring wind and her hair dishevelled. 'Sorry, am I late?'

Gwen looked at her watch. 'Yes,' she said and the girl slunk behind her desk. Gwen turned to Annabel. 'I'm going to lunch now—hungry?'

'I'm not going until I've seen Mr Jerrard,' Annabel said defiantly and got a wry smile.

'He won't be back for hours, but suit yourself.' She walked back into the inner office and returned a few moments later wearing a camel-hair jacket. Annabel had had time to realise how hungry she was and to decide that she had been over hasty in refusing Gwen's tacit invitation.

'I would like some lunch,' she said apologetically and Gwen eyed her with sardonic amusement. Annabel was rather glad she didn't work with the older woman; Gwen was obviously an office tyrant, but just as obviously she knew Sam Jerrard very well and if carefully handled might give Annabel some tips on how to deal with him.

They ate at a small restaurant just around the corner. It was a quarter to two by the time they sat down at a table and the place was half-empty. Gwen advised her that the best item on the menu was the salad.

'As it doesn't need cooking, there's nothing they can do to that,' she said with the waitress eavesdropping shamelessly and glaring at them.

While they were eating the crisp, lightly dressed vegetables, Gwen asked, 'What on earth made you want to work in a laboratory? You don't look the type.'

'It seemed more interesting than working in an office, and there was little choice around Blackstone. Norfolk isn't a high employment area.'

Gwen nodded admission. 'I still think I'd get bored; there's something very off-putting about the atmosphere in those places. Don't you get scared when your young man is doing one of his experiments?'

'I was scared last time. It was the biggest bang of all, but Charlie seems to have a charmed life. He walked out of it with just a few scratches from flying glass. You know, this research if his *is* brilliant; on paper it's very exciting but of course he has to back up the theory with practical demonstrations and he hasn't quite got the exact proportions right. But he's done all the important work, he's just putting the finishing touches to it now, and if Mr Jerrard fires him and holds on to his research project, giving it to someone else to finish, it will be grossly unfair to Charlie. The credit should all go to him, but he won't get it if he's left Jerrard's.'

Earnestly, Annabel fixed Gwen Bridge with beseeching eyes. 'You do see, don't you?'

Gwen ate a slice of cucumber thoughtfully. 'What a pity he's so good at the theory and so ham-fisted when it comes to the practical side of research,' she agreed.

'Nobody's perfect. I realise Mr Jerrard must be furious now, but if I could only get him alone for half an hour and talk to him, I'm sure he'd have to see how very unfair he's being.'

Gwen's eyes were ironic. 'I wouldn't bank on it. Sam's already considering who should take over the project.'

'Oh, he can't do that!' Agitated, Annabel shifted on her chair, green eyes glittering with anger. 'If I sit in that waiting room for a week, I'm going to see him!'

'I'm afraid he's flying to Brussels on Monday and he'll be away for a fortnight.' Gwen finished her salad and surveyed her with a smile. 'Sorry.'

'Then I must see him this afternoon.'

'He won't be back from lunch until getting on for four, I'd say, and he's leaving early to spend the weekend down at his cottage in Norfolk.'

Annabel's eyes lit up. 'Norfolk? Where?'

'I've no idea. I don't know the address. All I have is the phone number and that's ex-directory so you couldn't check the address from that.' Gwen smiled at her. 'I can tell you one thing—it's nowhere near Blackstone, that I do know, because I assumed it was at first, but Sam told me it was a good hour's drive from the labs. I think he deliberately bought a place out of reach of the lab when he was working there himself. He wanted somewhere remote and peaceful where he couldn't be reached. I'm strictly forbidden to give out his phone number except in a real emergency.' She grinned. 'When your boyfriend blows up the lab for instance.'

The waitress removed their plates. 'Coffee?' she asked and they both nodded.

'If I could only get him alone for half an hour, make him listen!' Annabel muttered.

'Half an hour wouldn't do it,' Gwen advised. 'You need a whole day, at least.' She was laughing but Annabel wasn't amused.

'I mean it!'

Gwen stopped laughing and studied her with sharp interest. 'Have you got a car? You could always follow him down to the cottage.'

Annabel groaned. 'I came by train, damn it.'

The waitress appeared with their bill and Annabel took it from her. 'I'll pay,' she insisted and after a brief argument Gwen accepted the offer with a smile.

As they walked back she said, 'If you're lucky, Sam won't appoint anyone to take over the project until he gets back from Brussels,' then laughed, giving Annabel a wry glance. 'You're very persuasive, you've got me half-convinced against my better judgment. I can see why your young man sent you to talk Sam around.'

'Could you talk to Mr Jerrard, persuade him to see me?' Annabel asked quickly and Gwen ruefully surveyed her, shaking her head.

'In the mood Sam's in, I'd get nowhere.' She pushed open the swing doors, giving the receptionist a sharp look. The girl was typing busily now but had all too obviously just begun work again. Gwen walked past her, vanishing, and Annabel sat down to wait, an eye on her watch.

It was almost four when she heard the lift stop at that floor and when Sam Jerrard did appear he had Denise Keiron with him. Annabel had turned eagerly, but her face fell as she recognised the blonde girl. Today, Denise was wearing a white mink jacket over a chic, black dress. Annabel saw the glint of gold around her throat, the flash of diamonds in her small ears, and ferociously wished her at the other end of the earth. She wouldn't get Sam Jerrard's attention while Denise Keiron was around.

'Still here?' Sam Jerrard drawled, giving Annabel a sardonic smile as he passed, but he didn't stop. Denise apparently didn't see her at all; she moved beside him with that swaying walk as if everyone else in the room was beneath her notice.

The receptionist sighed, turning to stare after them, and when they had vanished said to Annabel, 'Did you see that mink? She's gorgeous, isn't she? I wonder what it's like to be that rich? Her father's on our board now—they say Mr Jerrard's going to marry her and I hope he does. That will put old Gwen's nose out of joint; she won't be able to act as if she owned him then, will she?'

Annabel didn't have time to answer. Gwen appeared again and the receptionist did her busy act under that basilisk stare. Gwen was not alone;

Denise Keiron was walking after her, talking in a clear, peremptory voice.

'How dare you speak to me like that? Who do you think you are? Give me that number immediately or I'll have to speak to my father.'

'If Mr Jerrard instructs me to give you his private number, I'll certainly do so,' Gwen said stiffly.

'*I'm* instructing you to tell me,' snapped the other girl. 'My father is one of the firm's directors, have you forgotten that?'

'Not at all, Miss Keiron. I'm very sorry, but I have my orders and if I disobey Mr Jerrard I shall be in trouble.'

The blonde swung round on her, icy hauteur in her stare. 'If you annoy me, you'll be in trouble, I promise you. Mr Jerrard has asked me to marry him.' She fixed Gwen with a glittering eye. 'Now, give me that number.'

Gwen's lips thinned. She shook her head.

'You'll be sorry about this,' Denise Keiron promised her, walking away quivering with outrage. The swing doors swished behind her, catching her mink as it sailed out of sight. Watching with riveted fascination, Annabel saw her turn, glowering, and give the jacket a furious yank before walking into the waiting lift.

Beginning to laugh, Annabel looked at Gwen, but there was no answering amusement in the older woman's thin face. She was visibly in a temper, a white line drawn around her mouth. Walking past Annabel she said curtly, 'Come out here, I want to talk to you.'

Annabel followed reluctantly, wondering if

Gwen was going to try to throw her out. She found the secretary standing beside the lift, watching it fixedly. Denise was on her way down; they heard the whine of the machinery. Gwen looked round at Annabel. 'If you're determined to talk to Sam, there's one way you could do it. His car's in the basement car park. I've got the keys. We had to load some equipment in his boot and I haven't given the keys back to him yet. If you hid in the back of the car, he might not notice you until he got down to his cottage. Of course, when you appeared, he'd be furious, but at least you'd get your chance to make him listen.'

Annabel's mouth dropped open. She couldn't believe her ears. Why was Gwen offering to help her?

The secretary watched her, reading the suspicion and wariness in Annabel's face. Turning away, she shrugged. 'Oh, forget it—it's a crazy idea, anyway! I shouldn't have suggested it, but that blonde barracuda put my back up and . . . I must have been out of my mind.'

Annabel caught her arm as the secretary was about to go back into the reception lobby. 'I think it's a great idea, and I'll do it like a shot!'

Gwen hesitated, frowning. 'If he finds you, don't tell him I helped you because I'll deny it.' She pulled free. 'Oh, no, I can't do it . . . he'd kill me!'

'I won't breathe a word, he'll never know. Please, don't back out now.' Annabel pressed the lift button, holding Gwen's arm tightly, and when the lift arrived, she pulled Gwen, still faintly protesting, into it. As they descended, Gwen moaned, 'I know I'm going to regret this!'

The car park was very dark; a few overhead lights gave a fuzzy yellow glow which only intensified the shadows thronging the concrete cavern. The place had an air of menace. Gwen walked to a big, black estate car, but Annabel held back. She suddenly had cold feet again. She felt uneasy—why was Gwen really helping her? Had Denise bruised her ego so much that she was hitting back at Sam?

'What's the matter? Changed your mind?' Gwen turned back to her, looking doubtful.

'No!' Annabel said at once, contrarily determined to go through with it at this sign that Gwen, too, had cold feet. Sam Jerrard had brushed her off again this afternoon, walking past her with that superior blonde on his arm—somehow or other, he was going to be forced to listen to her!

'Remember, I know nothing about it—the car was unlocked and . . .'

'Don't worry, I'll say you showed me out of the front door and I came in again through the car park entrance and noticed his car.' Annabel climbed into the back of the car, which was very roomy and had high-backed front seats which she thought would give her plenty of cover. Did it matter why Gwen was doing this? Everyone had a motive and it wasn't often easy to guess the right one.

'He shouldn't be long,' Gwen said, hesitating with a hand on the door. 'Good luck.' The door slammed and Annabel heard her walk away, her footsteps ringing on the concrete. When the sound had died away, the place seemed horribly dark and empty. She hoped Sam Jerrard would come soon—she didn't want her resolve to weaken and it might if she had much time to think. She found a car rug on the back seat and pulled it over herself—when she heard Sam coming she would whisk it over her head and lie down flat. What if he looked into the back of the car and found her? What if Gwen had second thoughts and told him Annabel had hidden in his car? She still felt distinctly uncertain about the secretary; there was something very odd about Gwen's sudden offer of help.

The next half hour dragged; she almost fell asleep in the stuffy, dark car, and was actually nodding with drooping lids when she heard the crisp clip of feet moving towards her. Hands suddenly shaky, she pulled the rug over herself and crouched right down. A key was inserted into the lock of the door, then there was a pause. Sam Jerrard must be realising that the door hadn't been locked.

Hardly breathing, Annabel listened as he walked around the car. What was he doing? Oh, no, he's going to look in here, she thought, heart jumping about inside her like a frog, but he walked past and opened the boot. During the next moment Annabel perspired anxiously. Why did I say I'd do this? I must be mad. Maybe I ought to get out now and take whatever he chucks at me—he's going to be furious when I do get out. Oh, why on earth am I here?

She heard the boot slam down then the sound of footsteps on the concrete. The feet paused beside the back seat door. Annabel shut her eyes, as though that might make her invisible.

She felt Sam Jerrard looking into the back of the car but his glance was a brief one, a second later he was walking on and getting into the driver's seat.

The car engine fired, the wheels grated on the concrete and a moment later they were moving up a ramp and Annabel saw light through the woollen weave of the rug over her head. Nervous panic and exhaustion made her so tired that she closed her eyes again, although she fought the temptation of sleep in case she made some sound or movement which might alert Sam Jerrard.

He had wound the window down beside him; the roar of traffic was so deafening that Annabel risked a few careful movements to make herself more comfortable, coiling her legs under the passenger seat next to Sam and resting her head on a large book which had been dropped on to the floor.

The next thing she knew was a loud crash. Annabel had been dreaming: not a pleasant dream. She had dreamt that she was going to have her head cut off; she was kneeling down with her neck laid across a block. It was very uncomfortable but the thought of what was coming next made her cry out, 'No!'

She woke up with a start, confused for one second as she opened her eyes but remembering where she was almost at once. The car was no longer moving. The engine had been switched off. She heard the grate of feet on gravel outside the car and as she pulled back the rug she smelt the sea. There was no mistaking that strong salty smell of seaweed and water, or the sound of waves and wind.

Carefully raising her head, she caught sight of Sam Jerrard's tall figure some feet away. He was standing in a small porch now, unlocking the front door of a cottage. He disappeared inside it and Annabel's eyes skimmed curiously over the façade of the place. It was small, painted white, with two storeys but only two windows on each floor, and it stood alone in a small garden. From the look of the cottage she guessed it had been built around a century ago, probably as a labourer's cottage. Two rooms up, two rooms down, she thought. The windows were typically small, giving little light to the low-ceilinged rooms behind them, no doubt.

She gratefully stretched her cramped limbs and wriggled out of the car, a hand massaging her neck. That book had dug a painful ridge into her flesh. That's why I dreamt I was having my head cut off, she thought, wryly amused, as she looked around her. The sun had set, the dusk was falling. Looking at her watch she was appalled to see that it was half-past seven. Why had they taken so long to get here?

It made her nervous to realise that there was no other building in sight. Gwen had said that the cottage was isolated. She hadn't said it was miles from anywhere else. All Annabel could see was the grey, cloudy sky pressing low over fields of rough pasture in which she glimpsed the white, ambling shapes of sheep. She couldn't see the sea and realised it must be somewhere below them—the cottage was on some cliffs. Where exactly was she? she wondered.

At that moment, Sam Jerrard walked out of the cottage and stopped dead as he saw her. Annabel defiantly watched the rapid flash of reactions in his hard face; suprise, disbelief, bewilderment, followed unmistakably by rage.

'What the hell are you doing here?' he demanded in a voice that made her wince. 'How did you get here?' He looked around, as though expecting to see another car, those icy grey eyes searching the empty, dusky landscape.

'I came with you,' she admitted in a voice she tried to keep steady.

He stared, his black brows a straight and angry line above his eyes. 'With me?' he repeated, then looked at his car. 'In my car?'

'On the floor in the back seat,' she whispered, hoping he wasn't going to turn violent. He looked as if he might.

His voice was deep and only just under control. 'You hid in my car? When? When it was in the car park? How did you know it was mine?' He grimaced. 'You've seen it when I come to the lab, I suppose?' His hands were thrust into his pockets; she hoped they would stay there. Across the space between them she got a sharp impression of anger; if those hands emerged she suspected he might try to strangle her with them.

'It wasn't locked so I got into the back,' Annabel faltered. 'I had to talk to you—look, I know you must be angry, but this seemed the only way of getting your attention. Please, just listen to me for a few minutes.'

'No, you listen to me, you obstinate little pest!' he interrupted, his face dark with fury. 'I don't want to hear another word about Draycott. Do you have any idea how much damage he did this

time? Have you any notion how much it will cost
to replace all the equipment he blew up? That lab
will be out of commission for weeks, holding up
that entire project. I blame myself for letting him
carry on working for me as long as I did.'

She opened her mouth and he took three long
strides until they were only inches apart. 'Not
another word!' he roared, bending towards her,
and she jumped visibly, eyes widening.

There was a little silence during which she heard
her own quick, stricken breathing. Eyes lowered,
she whispered, 'Then I'd better leave, I suppose.'

'How?' he asked curtly and she looked up in
bewilderment.

'I'll ring Charlie—he'll come and fetch me.'

'He won't, because you aren't ringing him, not
from here. This is my private hide-away. I've kept
the address a secret for five years, I don't want
anyone at Jerrard's to know where to find me when
I'm here, and I'm not breaking my rule for you.
You got yourself here without my help, you can
get yourself back the same way.'

The wind threw a thick strand of red hair across
her eyes and she pushed it back with a shaky hand.
'Well, will you ring for a taxi for me, then, please?'

'No,' he said and walked past her to open the
boot and lift out several boxes. He walked past her
back into the cottage and she looked around,
suddenly aware that darkness had completely
engulfed the countryside. How far was it to the
nearest village? she wondered. Oh, she must have
been mad to get herself into this mess!

Sam Jerrard came back while she was still
hesitating and looked at her with grim irony.

'Still here? You *are* hard to get rid of. If you're planning to walk, you ought to get moving soon or it will be pitch black out there, and there's no straight road to the nearest village. The roads here wind all over the place and the signposts are no help; they all point to Norwich and never mention anywhere else. If you get lost, you could end up falling over a cliff, and even if you manage to take the right roads it's still a six-mile walk. They'll let you ring from the only pub and it's warm in there—they have a real fire in the public lounge. That's if they're still open by the time you get there. How fast can you walk?'

Annabel was trembling with rage, very flushed and on the point of hitting him.

'I don't think you're funny,' she muttered, hands screwed at her sides.

He stood in front of her, a very tall, hard man with eyes that made her feel like a silly child.

'That makes two of us, then, Miss Walsh. Did you expect me to be thrilled to see you? You over-estimate your attractions.'

Her colour grew hotter. 'I just wanted to talk to you about Charlie. Why couldn't you listen, for a few minutes? I was desperate.'

'He doesn't deserve your brand of loyalty—he's a fool,' Sam Jerrard said between tight lips.

'No, he isn't, he's very clever, but he has a fatal flaw, that's all . . .'

'The word fatal is at least apt.'

'I thought,' she said hurriedly, trying to get her plea in before he could stop her, 'that if Charlie handled the theoretical side and somebody else did all the practical experiments there'd be no more trouble.' She stopped, aware that he was listening, his cold eyes intent. 'I didn't want you to appoint someone else to the project before I'd had a chance to suggest it.'

'The someone else who would do all the practical work being you, I take it?' he murmured and she looked away.

'I'd be glad to, but if you preferred someone else . . .'

Sam Jerrard looked at his watch. 'I don't know about you, but I'm hungry and tired. While I finish unpacking my gear, will you go into the kitchen there and make a pot of tea? I've put a hamper on the kitchen table. I brought down some cheese, bread and fruit and some tins of soup. Could you start laying a meal?'

Annabel hesitated. 'Of course but . . .'

He lifted one brow. 'But?'

'Afterwards . . . would you run me to the next village, please? Then I can ring Charlie from there.' She tried a little humour, smiling coaxingly at him. 'And I won't be in danger of falling over any cliffs.'

He smiled back, but with a cool mockery she did not like. 'Oh, no, Miss Walsh, I'm afraid not. I'm not driving anywhere tonight. I'm going to have a meal, then I'm going to bed. I want to be up at six tomorrow to do some photography on the cliffs; the best time to get pictures of the gulls nesting is just as dawn is breaking, and I fully intend to get a good night's sleep before I have to get out there.' His eyes were the colour of dawn frost as he watched her. 'So you have an interesting choice in front of you—you can either walk until you find a village, or you can stay here the night—there's only one bedroom upstairs, and only one bed. I'll be using that, but you're welcome to share it.' He watched the flare of red rise in her face. 'Otherwise, there's a couch in the sitting room. I can spare you a pillow and a couple of blankets.'

He turned to walk back to the house. Annabel got her breath back as he was moving through the front door.

'I can't stay here all night,' she threw after him and she heard him laugh.

'You should have thought of that before you stowed away in my car.'

CHAPTER THREE

ANNABEL walked shakily into the kitchen and
began to unpack the small rush hamper she found
on the table. She couldn't believe he meant it. He
surely wouldn't force her to spend the night here,
alone with him? He must be tormenting her
because she had made a nuisance of herself. She
could understand how irritating it must be to have
come all this way for some peace and quiet only to
find yourself saddled with an uninvited guest, but
it wouldn't take up more than half an hour of his
time to run her to the nearest village, would it?

She looked at the assembled items she had
placed on the table: a large chunk of Stilton, some
apples and oranges and a stick of French bread
and three cans of vegetable soup. If this was all he
had brought down for the weekend, he must eat
sparingly, or perhaps he mostly ate out? She heard
him going back upstairs, his step heavy, as though
he was carrying something large. She wasn't
surprised to hear that he was an amateur
naturalist; a good deal of the research the
laboratories carried out was connected with the
land, and she seemed to remember hearing that he
was from a farming family, although there were so
many rumours about him that it was difficult to
sort out the unlikely from the probable.

Sam Jerrard was the sort of man of whom
myths are made and to whom all sorts of stories

adhere, true or untrue. People talked about him; what they didn't know they invented and what they did know, they embroidered.

She put on the kettle and made tea, found a cupboard full of crockery and a drawer full of cutlery and laid the table, curious about the way he lived when he was here alone and impressed, if slightly reluctantly, by the neatness of the kitchen, the way everything had a place and was carefully put back in it after use. Or did he have some local cleaner who came in once he had gone back to London to tidy up? Annabel wished she could believe that, but she had a feeling Sam Jerrard always lived like this—with discipline and precision.

He closed the front door and Annabel jumped. She quickly set out the cups, her hands unsteady, and was just pouring the tea when he joined her.

He had shed his sheepskin coat and the jacket of his dark lounge suit. His hair was wind-blown and his face slightly flushed from the exertion of carrying heavy equipment up the stairs. His presence made the small kitchen shrink.

He went over to the kitchen sink and washed his hands, saying over his shoulder, 'It just began to rain—you'll have a wet walk if you go now.'

She looked quickly at the kitchen window and saw the dark streaks moving down the glass. Only then did her ears pick up the splash of water in the cottage gutters. Oh, damn, she thought, staring at the rainy windows, but on the other hand if it was raining Sam Jerrard wasn't going to be able to do much photography tomorrow morning, was he? That would mean that he wouldn't have to get up so early or go to bed so early, and he could run her to the next village.

Annabel carefully didn't say so. 'Your tea's ready,' she murmured, and he swung towards her, drying his hands. To her shock, she felt a peculiar flutter just below her rib-cage, as though a butterfly had been trapped there. She stared at him, eyes widening, and he stared back, a quizzical, puzzled expression in his face. Outside in the garden, rain drummed on the path. Annabel pulled herself together and sat down and Sam Jerrard walked over to sit down opposite her.

'Where's the soup?' he asked, looking over the sparsely laid table.

'Oh, I forgot it!' She began to get up and he put out a hand to stop her.

'Never mind, we'll just have bread and cheese.'

'Isn't that very indigestible at night?'

'It never keeps me awake, that's what I live on when I'm here. I haven't got time to cook.'

She wasn't hungry either. She took an orange and began to peel it while he ate some bread and a little cheese.

'During the week in London I eat too much, anyway. I spend too much time at business lunches,' Sam Jerrard said, his face wry. 'I often wish I could go back to the days when I worked at the laboratories myself; I had far more fun, the work's so absorbing.'

'Why don't you leave the business side to someone else and go back to the labs, then?'

His mouth twisted, anger and what might almost have been bitterness in the movement. 'That's impossible.' He looked at the fruit she was beginning to eat. 'If you want some soup, by all means have it.'

'No, it doesn't matter, I'm not hungry either.' She finished eating her orange and went over to the sink to wash her hands. Over her shoulder she asked, 'Why is it impossible for you to go back to working in the lab?'

He was silent and she turned to find him staring at her with hard, darkened eyes. 'You're as persistent as a gadfly,' he muttered. 'Don't you ever know when a subject is closed?'

'I didn't mean to be inquisitive,' she said, flushing. 'I'm so used to talking problems out with my brothers.' Then she froze, her mouth open in a gasp. 'Oh, I've forgotten! My brother! Joe will wonder where on earth I've got to—I'm supposed to be having dinner with him and his wife tonight; I'm staying at their flat this weekend.' She looked pleadingly at Sam. 'Could I just ring them and explain?'

He got up in an impatient movement, his body lithe under the white shirt. 'Do you think that would be a good idea? They'd be bound to ask questions about where you are and as you can't answer them it would only make matters worse.' He walked to the door. 'I'm going to bed.'

'You can't leave me,' she burst out and he looked round, his lids drooping and a little smile curling his mouth.

'You want to come, too? Why not?' His gaze wandered over her and her pulse went crazy with alarm. She backed until she was against the wall, breathing audibly.

'Don't make jokes like that, I don't think

they're funny.'

'Oh, it wasn't a joke,' he murmured, his voice deep with amusement. 'I ought to teach you not to leap before you look. Didn't it even enter your head that it might be foolhardy to strand yourself here with me? Some men might see it as an invitation they couldn't bear to refuse.' His lazy eyes moved from her wide stare to her parted, pink mouth down to the agitated rise and fall of her breasts under the shirt she wore. 'You're a very headstrong girl. Maybe I'd better disconnect the phone—and take you up to bed with me. I'm not sure I can trust you down here on your own.'

Her hand groped along the window-still and found a saucepan she had intended to use for the soup she had forgotten to heat. She grabbed the handle and Sam Jerrard began to laugh.

'And what are you going to do with that? Your taste for the dramatic verges on lunacy.' He turned and walked towards the door, saying over his shoulder, 'Amusing though you are, Miss Walsh, I still intend to get an early night, so I suggest you come and get the pillow and blankets and make yourself up a bed on the couch, down here. I'll be up before first light. I'll wake you then and drive you into St Audyn's—there's a bus from there to Norwich at six-thirty. It takes hours, of course, jolting from village to village, but perhaps it will teach you a lesson. You apparently don't mind inconveniencing other people, but perhaps you'll be less happy about inconveniencing yourself.'

Gritting her teeth, Annabel trudged after him, not daring to say anything else. Upstairs, he went into a bedroom and she stood on the landing, waiting. There were, as she had suspected, only two rooms upstairs—the door of the other room was open and inside she could see a wide range of scientific equipment: microscopes, a shelf crammed with labelled bottles and jars, cameras and boxes of slides, binoculars and a mounted telescope near the window, shelves of books and stacked notebooks.

Did he escape down here from the business grind of London to hours of scientific work? Puzzled, she stared into the room. Why couldn't he come back to the laboratories? Why was it impossible for him to hand over the business side to someone else? He had implied that she was insensitive to other people, but she had clearly picked up anger and frustration in him when he talked over supper.

As Sam Jerrard came towards her, his arms full of blankets with a pillow piled on top of them, she said apologetically, 'Sorry to be a nuisance . . .'

'Belated, but I accept the apology,' he said with dry irony.

'But . . .' she began, flushing again.

He sighed. 'But what, Miss Walsh? Don't start off about Draycott, again, because I have heard all I want to hear on that subject.'

'No, I was going to . . . well, I've been looking for a bathroom and there doesn't seem to be one.'

He waved a hand back into his bedroom. 'I'm afraid the only one is through here.'

Aghast, she stared, seeing a door on the far side of his bedroom. 'Isn't that very inconvenient?'

'As I intended the cottage solely for my own

use, no,' he said coolly. 'Look, I'll take these things downstairs and dump them on the couch in the sitting room while you use the bathroom.'

He walked past her and she cautiously entered his bedroom, listening to the drum of his feet on the stairs, while she looked around her in muted curiosity. The bedroom was as neat as all the other rooms: on each side of the bed a deep recess filled up with bookshelves, the carpet and curtains a restrained sage green and the walls painted with a paler green. Sketches of birds, flowers and boats; larger paintings of the sky and sea, hung along one wall. Annabel stared, sure that they had all been the work of one artist and wondering with sharp surprise if the artist was Sam Jerrard himself.

She didn't have time to look any closer. She wanted to use the bathroom and get out of here before Sam Jerrard came back, so she shot across the bedroom and bolted the bathroom door behind her. Everything, here, was spotless and tidy, too; a compact shower in a glass cubicle, a wash basin and a lavatory crammed into a tiny space, the way they were on a boat, she thought. Did Sam Jerrard sail? She suspected that he did. At least he liked boats—quite a few of the sketches on his bedroom wall had been of boats.

He was waiting when she emerged from the bathroom. 'I made up a bed for you,' he said, observing her scrubbed clean face with interest.

'Thank you,' she said, sidling towards the door like a crab. It made her nervous to be here in this room with him. The soft whisper of the rain outside made the atmosphere too intimate, reminding her that there was probably no other

living soul for miles; they were quite alone here in
the dark and the night.

'Good night,' he mocked, laughter below the
softness of his voice. 'Sure you won't change your
mind and stay with me?'

Annabel bolted for the stairs. She heard him
close his bedroom door and slowed, breathing less
hurriedly. His sense of humour annoyed her
almost as much as her own stupidity for having
got herself into this situation.

He had cleared the kitchen, washed up the few
plates they had used and put away the food. She
put off the light and went into the sitting room. It
was larger than she had expected. A bay window
had been thrown out on one side giving more
light, no doubt, although tonight the curtains were
drawn over it. Here, too, she found shelves of
books along one whole wall. There was an
expensive stereo unit built into a recess by the
stone fireplace. Above it hung a large oil painting
of a cottage, cliffs, a blue, cloudy sky. Annabel
stood in front of it, staring at the signature—a
hasty black scrawl with a paintbush. She wasn't
absolutely certain, but she thought the name was
Jerrard; it had been done so rapidly that she could
be wrong, though.

There was something familiar about the cottage.
She studied it, head to one side. Was it this one?
She had only seen the façade, briefly, in the falling
dusk, and couldn't be quite sure—but if it was this
cottage, then Sam Jerrard must surely have been
the painter? Her interest quickened, admiring the
way the half-open door showed a block of dark
blue shadow which suggested summer, a dim

mirror on a wall just inside the door revealing
something of the room beyond—a pink geranium
in a terracotta pot, a velvet-backed chair, a misty
shape which, her instincts told her, was probably a
woman, from the curve of the smiling mouth and
the wide, blue eyes. There they were, in the mirror,
artfully arranged in movement, living but caught
in spectral immobility as if they had all taken a
breath and frozen between one heartbeat and the
next. By some magic, the painter had painted more
than just a cottage—within the mirror was the life
led inside those walls, a trembling happiness
almost tangibly present.

Annabel couldn't help going closer to try to
decipher the features of the woman reflected in the
mirror, but the closer she got the more indistinct
the face became, dissolving into a whirl of
coloured dots of paint: green, white, pink.

Ruefully she stepped back and the face swam
out of dimness, smiling, mocking her attempt to
come any closer. It bore no resemblance to anyone
she had ever seen. She couldn't see the woman's
hair or what she wore; there was just a pale face,
eyes, a mouth. If Sam Jerrard had painted it, who
was the woman? she wondered, then caught herself
up, grimacing.

It was none of her business, was it? If the gossip
about him was accurate, there had been plenty of
women in his life in the past, perhaps still were?
There was nothing specific about the woman in the
painting, except that somehow Annabel got the
impression of warmth and happiness, but that
could be merely a matter of the light, the spray of
climbing roses near the cottage door, the blue sky

and the loving care with which the picture had been painted.

Deliberately turning away she began to browse along the bookshelves, looking for something to read. She knew she wasn't going to find it easy to get to sleep. It was early, for a start, and secondly she was rather uptight about being here at all. She was curious about Sam Jerrard's taste in books. She could be almost certain that the books in the spare room upstairs were all scientific, connected with his work. Down here, though, she found a wider range of reading material—from a fat tome on anatomy to a few dozen books on the fauna and flora of various countries as well as rows of detective stories, classic novels and biographies.

She picked one of these, a biography of one of her own heroines, the scientist Marie Curie, and then considered how she was going to sleep on the couch. She certainly wasn't taking off all her clothes. The question was: how many should she take off?

Sam Jerrard had promised—or threatened— whichever way you cared to look at it, to wake her up at first light. She didn't want him finding her half-naked. She ruefully decided she would sleep in her slip and bra and panties.

There was a lamp on a table next to the couch. She curled up under the blankets, glad of their warmth as the spring night grew chillier, and read until her eyes grew heavy, then switched off the lamp. Outside the rain was flung against the windows by a howling wind and the distant roar of the sea was louder; the tide must be in, she sleepily decided, and drifted into a deeper sleep to the lullaby of that pounding surf.

She woke again to a room full of spring sunshine and the smell of bacon and coffee. For a second or two, Annabel lay on the couch staring at the ceiling blankly until with a jerk of shock she realised where she was and sat up, the blankets falling on to the floor.

It was broad daylight; she knew before she looked at her watch that it must be very late. Sam Jerrard hadn't woken her as he promised; had he overslept too? It was almost nine o'clock and the rain had vanished. It was going to be a lovely day from the look of the blue sky, she thought, staring at the windows.

That was when she really woke up, staring at the opened curtains. They had been drawn last night. Someone had been in here while she slept and pulled them back, someone must have looked at her while she was blissfully unaware of being watched. She writhed in embarrassment, realising that. It was only human to hate the thought of being watched while one slept, off-guard and vulnerable, yet it was more than that—Annabel hated the thought of Sam Jerrard bending over her, looking at her, so skimpily clad and dishevelled in that makeshift bed. Even when she was wide awake the man unnerved her.

She slid off the couch, her short white slip rumpled after having been slept in, and hurriedly picked up her clothes from the chair where she had neatly folded them the night before. She was off balance, perhaps, because at her first grab the chair rocked and toppled over, and while she was picking it up she heard the door open.

Swinging round, wide-eyed and flushed, she broke out, 'Please, I'm not dressed!'

Sam Jerrard didn't go out again. He took his time inspecting her, those grey eyes openly speculative, as they moved from her smooth, bare shoulders over the very female curves of the body below them. Her skin began to burn. He didn't miss much. In leisurely curiosity his gaze visited every inch, from the generous cleft between her half-covered breasts, to her small waist and rounded hips, down over the slim thighs showing beneath the brevity of her slip. He didn't stop there. He went on down to her feet, making her so self-conscious that even the nakedness of her toes made her squirm.

'Well, you're awake at last!' he drawled.

'You promised to wake me as soon as it was light!' she accused and, since he showed no sign of moving, turned her back to slide into her clothes with fingers that fumbled.

'I tried,' he said. 'I came in and pulled the curtains and bent over and gave you a little shake but you were sleeping like the dead; you didn't even stir!'

She was glad he couldn't see her face—it might betray how disturbing she found it to know that he had looked at her so closely while she was asleep.

'You should have yelled,' she said, turning slowly once she was fully dressed. He gave her a mocking little smile, his eyes flicking down and up again, as though fully aware that she was fiercely relieved to be decently covered up, and amused by her shyness.

'I decided to make some coffee and wake you later,' he said, then paused, eyeing her. 'But first I went to get the car out of the garage, but I couldn't start it. There's something wrong with the damned thing; I'm afraid I won't be able to drive you along to the village for a while.'

Annabel couldn't believe her ears, her lips parting on a gasp of shock, and then as she took in what he had said she looked at him hard.

He watched the suspicion and incredulity grow in her face, his own eyes derisive.

'I know, it's almost beyond belief!'

'You don't expect me to *believe* it, do you?' she spat, the ruffled red hair bristling on the nape of her neck. 'I'm not that naïve.'

'I've rung the garage and they'll send a mechanic out in a couple of hours,' he said, ignoring her comment. 'I had a look at the engine myself and I couldn't see what was wrong; it's probably electrical. The garage is quite dry but as it was such a cold, wet night there may have been condensation inside the engine.'

'I can't hung around here for half the day,' Annabel said angrily. 'You've got to let me ring Charlie.'

He lifted his shoulders in an impatient shrug. 'First, I've just cooked breakfast—if you want some you'd better come and get it in five minutes or it will be uneatable.' He turned and walked out, vibrating almost visibly with irritation. She wondered if he had managed to get out to the cliffs and take pictures of his nesting gulls, or had he been trying to start his car since first light?

She ran upstairs into the bathroom and washed, cleaning her teeth with a spare toothbrush she found thoughtfully laid out, still in a wrapper.

As she went back through his bedroom she saw

that he had already made his bed; it was as smooth as glass. Sam Jerrard was as careful a housekeeper as her own mother, she thought, smiling, and with a sudden appetite she went downstairs again and smelt that delicious bacon.

He got her plate out from under the grill, where it had been keeping warm, and deftly slid it on to the table as she came into the kitchen, then resumed his seat opposite and poured himself more coffee before filling her cup.

'You're very domesticated,' Annabel said, staring with appreciation at her plate of perfectly cooked bacon, mushrooms and tomatoes.

'I learnt to be self-sufficient after I left home,' he said, finishing his meal with a slice of toast and marmalade. 'When I was at university and living in one room with a gas ring to cook on, it was obvious I had to learn to be tidy or live like a pig in a sty, so I trained myself to be tidy and to cook using just one pan. My mother was amazed. When I lived at home I never did a thing for myself. She waited on me hand and foot—a big mistake, I think, but she was another generation and she had been brought up to believe that men were helpless and too important to do such mundane things as make their own beds or cook.'

Annabel grimaced. 'She sounds like my mother. My brothers are pretty useless.'

He leaned back, watching her eat. 'How many have you got?'

'Brothers? Five.'

'Five?' His brows shot up. 'Good heavens—and how many sisters?'

'None, I'm the only girl.'

'Are they older or . . .'

'All older—I was the youngest.' She regretfully ate the last mushroom. 'That was the best breakfast I've had for years.' Looking up, she asked in sudden suspicion, 'Where did it all come from? I didn't see any bacon or mushrooms last night.'

'I got it from the milkman,' Sam Jerrard said, grinning. 'He doubles up as a grocer and greengrocer out here; his van carries a whole range of goods.'

'Van?' repeated Annabel. 'Van? I could have gone with him to the village, then! When did he call?'

'He didn't—I saw his van coming over the hill and ran across the cliffs catching him at the fork in the road. He doesn't call here unless I ring and ask him to and I only do that if I'm going to be here for more than a couple of days.'

Annabel drank her coffee, glowering. 'If I'd known, I could have waited for him on the road, though.'

'You could,' agreed Sam. 'But I forgot all about him. The milkman doesn't exactly dominate my thinking process. Sorry.'

'You're not sorry,' Annabel muttered.

Sam got up, his lean body forceful in the abrupt movement. 'No, that's right, I'm not,' he snarled. 'I didn't invite you here and as you got yourself here you can damn well get yourself back where you belong. I don't know why I'm bothering with you. Because of you I lost half the best part of the morning. By the time I got out on the cliffs the sun was up and most of the gulls were off their nests or too wide awake for me to get very close to them. I came down here for a couple of peaceful days. You've wrecked everything and after I've cooked you breakfast and tried to be tolerant about all the bother you've put me to, you sit there sulking like a schoolgirl. I ought to smack you.'

Alarmed, she shrank back against her chair. 'You just try!'

He took a step and she went rigid, but then Sam gave another low snarl, turning away. 'Don't worry, I don't get my kicks slapping women around, whatever the provocation! I'm going to take another look at my car; if it *was* condensation it may have dried out by now.'

Annabel watched him stride out, feeling petty and mean. She could hardly blame him for losing his temper; he hadn't asked to be saddled with her. Under the circumstances he had behaved pretty well, she had to admit. Some men might have taken advantage of the situation; stuck out here in the middle of nowhere in a cottage alone with her the temptation could have been irresistible.

She began to tidy the kitchen and wash up, then paused, realising that in some ways Sam Jerrard's gentlemanly restraint was less than a compliment. He hadn't really made so much as a pass—oh, a few teasing cracks about sharing his bed with her, and the odd glance of roving interest when he came into the room this morning and saw her in her slip and undies—but Annabel had had more pressing advances made by guys in far less intimate situations. She had been kissed over a bunsen burner and had a whispered suggestion made as she was looking through a microscope.

She knew several men who, left alone with her all night in a cottage, would have been ready to batter down the door to get at her. Of course, they were all men she detested, and she hadn't wanted Sam Jerrard to try anything on, but, all the same, she felt rather slighted.

Obviously, he didn't find her that alluring. Obviously, he had not been tempted. What's wrong with me? she thought, furiously cleaning the table. I'm not a blue-eyed blonde, I suppose. Is that his type? Presumably—and perhaps he really was in love with Denise Keiron. Annabel found his taste suspect. What did he see in the girl? She was rich and spoilt and had that expensive gloss which one could see in colour magazine photographs of the wealthy and well-groomed, but Annabel hadn't liked her, and neither, obviously, had Sam's secretary. Not surprisingly, after Denise Keiron threatened and insulted her! The way the girl had talked to Gwen Bridge had been so gratuitously unpleasant—it had left one with a far from complimentary impression of Denise Keiron's character.

Annabel looked around the kitchen. It was spotless again—she wasn't going to let Sam Jerrard think she was less domesticated than himself!

She walked through into the sitting room to gather up her tumbled blankets and the pillow she had used, made a neat pile of them and took them back upstairs to place them on the end of Sam's bed, then went back to restore the sitting room, too, to the state in which she found it.

While she was doing that she heard the distant

sound of a car engine and went to the window. This must be the garage mechanic. Sam was outside, his head out of sight in the lifted bonnet of his car. She saw him straighten, the black gleam of his hair catching the spring sunlight, then he stared, shading his eyes with one hand, stiffened and turned, beginning to run into the cottage.

The next second he burst through the sitting-room door and grabbed her arm. 'Quick, you've got to get out of sight!'

Annabel dug her heels in, resisting the drag on her arm. 'Why?' she asked suspiciously. 'What are you talking about?'

'I just saw Denise's car coming,' he grated in a hard, impatient voice. 'There's no mistaking the bloody thing—a damn great Rolls on these roads is like a dinosaur in Piccadilly. God knows how she got my address—if Gwen gave it to her, I'll kill her by inches.' He tightened his hold on Annabel. 'Come on! She'll be here any minute, and if she finds you here all hell will be let loose.'

CHAPTER FOUR

'I'M not scuttling out of sight like a mouse when the light goes on,' Annabel said indignantly, trying to pull herself free. 'Why should I hide?'

'Because if she finds you here at this hour of the morning the first thing she's going to ask is, how long have you been here? And when she finds out you've been here all night, we're both going to wish we'd never been born. Denise has a very nasty temper.'

Annabel could believe it. 'Can't we say I just arrived?' she asked.

'How did you get here?' he enquired, one eye on the window. Annabel could hear the Rolls clearly now; the purr of the engine sounded as though a panther had been let loose in the sunny landscape which had succeeded last night's storm. Sam looked back at her, his lip curling back from his teeth in a silent snarl. 'Damn you, get a move on! Believe me, if she sees you there will be trouble.'

'Are you engaged to her?' Annabel asked with a funny little clutch of anger in her stomach. It wasn't pain exactly, just an unpleasant sensation close to apprehension.

Sam said shortly, 'I've asked her to marry me, yes.'

They looked at each other in the brief stillness. Sam was frowning. Annabel was pale. She made no attempt to move; she wasn't thinking; she just looked at him with wide, uneasy green eyes and he stared back as if her silence said something more audible than words.

'All right, I'll give Draycott his job back,' he broke out. 'Will you please go upstairs and stay there until I can get Denise away from here?'

Annabel turned and ran. Sam might believe that she had been holding out as some sort of blackmail, but it wasn't that that had held her rooted to the spot. She had been overwhelmed by a totally primitive feeling of jealousy. It was crazy; she couldn't explain it even to herself. She hardly knew the man. It was none of her business if he meant to marry Denise Keiron. She wasn't in love with him—how could she be? Yet she couldn't pretend that she didn't know what was wrong with her even though she had never felt that particular violent emotion before. This knife-like twisting deep inside her was jealousy and as she dived into the bedroom upstairs she clenched her hands at her sides, trying to fight it down.

The Rolls had parked outside by the time she went to the window. Annabel saw Sam on the path talking to Denise and her father. Sam's voice floated up to her.

'How on earth did you manage to track me down?' He spoke lightly but Annabel heard the undertone of anger, even if Denise seemed unaware of it.

'Oh, we have our sources,' she was saying, laughing triumphantly. 'I've been dying to see your little hide-away—what do you do down here, for heaven's sake? What a dead and alive hole. Miles from anywhere. And such a tiny cottage, too, it looks as though there isn't room to swing a cat. I suspected you held orgies out here, you were so secretive. Have you got a harem locked upstairs?'

'Just a microscope,' Sam said, coolly.

Denise shivered, holding her mink closer around her throat. 'Aren't you going to ask us in, darling? It's freezing out here.'

'Of course. I'll make some coffee and then you can tell me how you got this address,' Sam said, turning back towards the cottage. 'You haven't had me shadowed, have you?'

Annabel heard the front door close and the sound of footsteps moving downstairs. 'I'd get claustrophobia in this place,' James Keiron said in a deep, rumbling voice. 'How many rooms are there?'

They all moved into the kitchen. She heard the door close behind them and their voices grew indistinct. She walked away from the window and sat on a chair near the bed, staring at the carpet. Had Gwen Bridge had the address all the time; had she given it to Denise?

But if she had the address, why had she lied? Why had she talked Annabel into stowing away in Sam's car, when it would have been so much easier for Annabel to go home by train and then drive over to the cottage next day to see Sam?

Annabel's forehead creased with doubt and suspicion. It was inexplicable. She couldn't understand why Gwen should have lied to her. Perhaps Denise had got the address in some other way? Perhaps Sam had guessed correctly—perhaps she had had him followed here.

My God, Annabel thought, going pink. What if whoever followed him saw me getting out of his car? But there hadn't been a soul in sight that day; she remembered distinctly standing outside the cottage, staring around and seeing and hearing nothing but the wind in the trees and the soft swell of the sea.

Suddenly she heard the kitchen door open and the sound of voices again. She stiffened, listening. Were they going? Had Sam managed to talk them into leaving?

'I'll just go and see that everything's tidy,' Sam said, his voice very loud. 'There's nothing much to see upstairs, anyway—just my bedroom and a workroom.'

Annabel heard the submerged note of agitation in his voice and looked around the room desperately. Where on earth could she hide?

'No, I want to see it exactly as it is,' Denise insisted.

They were coming up; Annabel heard the stairs creaking. She moved towards the bathroom but Denise was sure to look at that—Annabel knew she would. Women always liked to look at the kitchen and bathroom of someone else's house.

She shot a hunted look around and then with a stifled groan got down and rolled under the bed, feeling like someone in a French farce. The pleated valance falling on each side should hide her, so long as Denise didn't stoop down to check under the bed, which she surely wouldn't do in Sam's bedroom while he stood there watching?

A second later the door was pushed wide and she heard them. 'It's rather stark, darling,' Denise said, laughing. Her laughter was as phoney as her smiles, Annabel thought with venom. 'Easy to see a man chose the furnishings. What a poky little window, too. These rooms are so gloomy, such low ceilings. But don't you keep them clean and tidy? Do you have someone from the village coming in to clean for you? All these pictures must be great dust-catchers—oh, I suppose you did them? Aren't you clever?' There was a little silence; through the gap between the valance and the carpet, Annabel could just see her white heels. She was standing mere inches from Annabel, who tried to breath silently and prayed she would not sneeze or cough.

'You're quite good, you know,' Denise said patronisingly. 'You ought to branch out into real painting soon—these sketches are all very well, but nobody cares much about sketches of birds; I mean, everyone does them, don't they? You ought to do some portraits—why don't I pose for you? I'm sure you'd do a very good portrait of me, and Daddy would buy it.'

'I don't think I'm ready to move on to portrait painting yet,' Sam said in a terse way. Was he looking around to see where Annabel was hiding?

'Don't be modest, darling. You could do it,' Denise said. 'You sound very uptight—are you waiting for my answer?'

Sam sounded uneasy, as well he might—he must be on tenterhooks in case Annabel suddenly appeared and blew this whole scene sky-high. She was almost tempted to do it, too, but she stayed where she was, an unwilling eavesdropper as Denise laughed softly, when Sam muttered, 'Yes, of course . . .'

'I've talked to Daddy and he's on your side, he likes the idea.' Denise suddenly sat down on the bed and Annabel jumped as the springs gave above her with a creak. 'Come and sit here, darling,' Denise invited huskily.

'Your father will be getting bored,' Sam said. 'Shouldn't we go down again?'

'Silly,' Denise murmured. 'Daddy will guess what we're up to.'

Annabel saw the other girl's white shoes tumble across the carpet and heard the bedsprings go again. My God, she's lying down! she thought, aghast, her face crimson as she realised what might happen next.

'You look very sexy in that sweater,' Denise purred. 'Come and kiss me or I'll get cross.'

Annabel put a hand over her mouth as she felt a hysterical giggle trying to force it sway out. She wished she could see Sam's face. She was almost sorry for him, knowing that she was listening to this and no doubt wishing her at the other end of the earth. She heard him move, slowly, and then heard the sound of a kiss, horribly audible and going on for far too long, she felt.

'What's the matter with you?' Denise whispered. 'Do you call that a kiss? Are you sulking because I found out where you hide yourself at weekends?'

'How *did* you find out?' Sam asked quickly.

'I'm not telling,' she retorted. 'You aren't the only one who can be secretive. I was suspicious when you kept going off and refusing to tell me where—I thought you might have another girl tucked away, and I wasn't going to get engaged to you until I was sure you wouldn't be two-timing me.'

Sam's voice was cool. 'I told you I came here to work in private.'

'Yes, darling, you did—but how did I know you weren't lying?'

'You could have tried trusting me,' Sam said flatly.

Denise laughed. 'You *are* sulking. Don't scowl at me like that. I talked to Daddy about it and he agreed that we ought to check you out ...'

'Check me out?' Sam's voice went up several decibels. 'Do you mean you've had me investigated?'

Denise's weight shifted on the bed; Annabel could see the faint indentation of her body where the springs sagged slightly. There was a deeper sag beside that; Sam was heavier than the blonde girl.

'Don't make a big thing of it,' Denise said quickly. 'All I meant was that we asked around ... now, Sam, be sensible, what would you think if you found out that I went off somewhere every weekend and wouldn't tell you where? Wouldn't you be just the tiniest bit suspicious?'

Put like that, it was understandable, Annabel thought, reluctantly.

She felt Sam get up. 'I think we'd better go back to your father,' he said walking to the door. His voice was deep and hard; he was angry and Denise recognised it. She got up, too, and slid her feet into her white shoes before following him. Annabel heard her talking coaxingly as she went.

'I'm sorry if I've hurt your feelings by not trusting you, Sam,' she murmured. 'You can't blame me, you know—you have quite a reputation as a lady-killer; don't pretend you don't know that. I don't mind about the past—I don't expect to be the first woman in your life any more than you're the first man in mine. We've both been around, haven't we? But marriage is something else again. Maybe I'm old-fashioned, but I expect to be the only woman in my husband's life.'

Her voice died away as they moved down the stairs. Annabel waited until they were out of earshot altogether before she rolled out from under the bed and got up. Her skirt was dusty and she bent to brush it, her face flushed.

She could see now why Sam had made her hide. If Denise had found her there she wouldn't have listened to any explanations and when Annabel mentally thought over what he would have said to the other girl she realised just how lame and improbable it would have sounded. She might not like Denise Keiron much but, looking at the situation from the other girl's point of view, she had to admit Denise had some justice on her side. Sam's secrecy must have seemed odd, and Annabel didn't know if it was so very old-fashioned to expect to be the only woman in one's husband's life—if it was, Annabel was old-fashioned too, and didn't care who knew it.

She avoided looking in the direction of the bed and walked towards the window. What was she to do now? How long would Denise and her father stay?

I'm not skulking about up here for hours, she promised herself, scowling. Yet how was she going to get away without risking being seen?

A gull shrieked over the cliffs and she jumped, gasping. Her nerves were shot to pieces. Just remembering the embarrassment of being forced to eavesdrop on the lovers made her face burn again. She put her hands to it, furious with herself.

Was Sam really in love with that girl? The question formed itself before she could silence it and she swung away, catching sight of herself reflected in a mirror on the far side of the room. Her face looked unfamiliar; skin hot, eyes hectic. What she saw worried her so much that she felt like rushing down the stairs and out into the clean, spring air. She wished she had never come here, never taken Gwen Bridge's advice, never stowed away in Sam's car. She had brought all this on herself.

She turned and leaned against the window, yearning like a trapped bird to escape through the impervious glass. It was only a few hours since she had first entered this cottage, but she felt as though in that short time she had suffered some devastating change, had been through something as explosive as one of Charlie's experiments.

The sound of voices below broke her into her angry self-absorption. Looking down quickly she saw James Keiron waddling towards the white Rolls. His daughter was close behind him, her blonde hair given a silvery sheen in the sunlight.

Annabel backed out of sight before she caught sight of Sam. She didn't want to be seen now—not after she had gone to so much trouble not to be caught. She heard their voices murmuring but couldn't distinguish what was being said. Sam's tone was still deep and harsh and Annabel thought that Denise's voice held a note of conciliation—or had they already made up their little quarrel?

What if Sam went with them? Annabel suddenly thought anxiously. She would then be stranded here unless she walked to the nearest village, and that would take hours.

At one time she had begun to doubt Sam Jerrard's insistence that the cottage was miles away from any village, but he had obviously been telling the truth from what Denise and her father had been saying. They had been disgusted by the remoteness of the place, hadn't they? In fact, they hadn't liked anything about Sam's secret retreat, which Annabel found baffling, because however inconvenient to her this isolated location was she couldn't help being drawn to the silence and beauty of the surroundings—the elms she saw from the window, still showing their flowers, an almost purple haze glowing against the leafless branches; the hazels closer at hand, leaning together in a little coppice, already in leaf but from their branches the last lambs tails drooping, shedding pollen in a pink dust whenever the wind shook their branch; the gulls wheeling overhead with white breasts and iridescent wings; the clear blue of the sky seemingly endless and without depth. She could see nothing ugly from that window, which was rare enough these days, she thought, grimacing.

The Rolls had moved off now. She risked peering out of the window, wondering if Sam had gone too, but his tall figure stood on the path, his black hair ruffled, his shoulders hunched against the wind, his hands in his pockets.

Annabel contemplated him with wry sympathy
—he looked fed up. Her brothers had given her
a shrewd idea of the way the male mind works.
She knew that any of her brothers would have died
rather than go through the scene which had been
played out upstairs in the cottage a few minutes
ago. Unless Sam Jerrard was a most unusual man,
embarrassment horrified him. He was probably
not looking forward to facing her again after what
she had overheard.

She went downstairs and Sam came slowly
through the front door as she reached the hallway.
Their eyes met; she saw his face tighten.

'For five years I've managed to keep this place a
secret,' he said harshly, 'then suddenly people keep
turning up out of the blue—I might as well sell it
now before I get whole busloads of tourists
demanding a guided tour.'

Annabel had intended to be diplomatic, but his
aggression somehow fed her own. 'Don't shout at
me!' she threw back. 'It wasn't my fault your
fiancée tracked you down. Anyway, did you think
you could stop her finding out about this place for
ever? Even after you were married?'

He looked stunned; she saw that that hadn't
occurred to him. Surely he hadn't imagined that a
wife would let him have a secret hide-away to
which she was never invited?

'You don't know much about women,' she said
and he snarled.

'I know something about blackmail.'

She stiffened. 'I didn't blackmail you—you
offered to give Charlie his job back if I helped you
out by hiding!'

'If you hadn't stowed away in my car, there wouldn't have been any need for you to hide!'

'If your fiancée trusted you,' Annabel said icily, 'we could have told her the truth about why I'm here.'

'No woman would have believed it,' Sam said with grating rage and Annabel paused to consider that, and to admit that he might well be right. Would she have believed him if she had been Denise?

He stared at her, his mouth a straight line, then asked, 'Which reminds me—where *were* you hiding?'

Annabel looked down, face demure, lashes a darkened fan across her cheek. 'Under the bed.'

There was a silence which throbbed unmistakably with violence. She looked through her lashes, her mouth quivering with silent laughter.

'Damn you!' Sam said through his teeth, dark red along his cheekbones. The laughter escaped and Sam took two steps to grab her shoulders, shaking her furiously. 'Don't laugh at me, you little witch!'

Her red hair floated out around her face, bright tendrils of living fire which clung to his warm skin as it brushed the hands gripping her. Her lashes were up again, showing him teasing green eyes full of laughter, into which he stared with fixity. He stopped shaking her and she stood motionless, suddenly alarmed by something in his hard face. She felt giddy, as if she had just stepped off a fair roundabout after spinning round and round with music playing. Her ears drummed with the echo of it and her lips parted on a gasp.

Sam's eyes drifted downwards from the dilated green eyes over the small, finely shaped nose to those quivering pink lips, the pulse of her emotions showing in the way they curved. His thumb caressed that female line while she stared up at him, unable to break away. His anger seemed to have dissipated; his lids were heavy over almost sleepy eyes, a languor in both of them which had the sensual warmth of some tropical night.

Sam very slowly lowered his head and her throat arched in a movement too instinctive to be checked, her pulsing mouth offered and taken in that languorous silence.

Annabel closed her eyes, concentrating everything in her on that slow kiss—nothing else existed. She felt she had been moving towards this moment since the day she was born, and yet oddly that she had experienced it a million times before. It had the shock and familiarity of sunrise or laughter—always new, however often it recurred. She knew the firm line of his back, that tapering spine, those strong muscular shoulders; she knew the way his skin felt roughly moving against her own; she knew the fresh salty smell of his skin and the living vibrancy of his thick black hair when her fingers touched it.

Sam pulled back, breathing unevenly and she was free, but she was cold and trembling in that freedom, looking at him with black-pupilled, frightened eyes. Did he know what had just happened to her? Had he realised the sort of impact his kiss had had?

Sam said huskily, 'You asked for that,' as if expecting her to slap him or start to scream.

Did I? she thought dazedly, flinching—did my eyes beg him to kiss me? Hot colour moved beneath her skin and she instinctively reached for anger, it was the safest emotion available to her now.

'If you like to think so!' she spat back.

'It may teach you not to laugh at men! I never intended to kiss you, I was going to slap you for a minute but the kiss seemed a better idea.' He looked faintly bewildered, as though he was more surprised than she was and couldn't understand what had happened.

'I think I'd have preferred the slap,' Annabel muttered, lying through her teeth. Obviously Sam hadn't found their kiss the same world-shaking experience she had; to him it had merely been a kiss delivered as a punishment because she had laughed at him. Hadn't Denise Keiron said that he had quite a reputation as a lady-killer? How many other women had he kissed like that? Annabel gritted her teeth; she didn't want to know.

'Just as well your fiancée didn't walk in just now,' she said nastily and saw him grimace.

As if in answer to her, they both heard the distinct note of a car engine moving along the lane and Sam swore under his breath.

'My God! What now?'

They stared at each other, their eyes exchanging the same thought—had Denise come back? Annabel said furiously, 'I am not hiding under that bed again!' and Sam pushed past her to look out of the door, his body relaxing again as he saw the vehicle approaching.

'It's okay, it's the breakdown truck—the

mechanic's coming to fix my car.' He went out, closing the front door behind him and Annabel weakly tottered into the kitchen to make herself a much-needed cup of coffee. She sat at the table to drink it a few moments later, staring out of the small kitchen window at the golden blaze of daffodils massed in the garden which, she suddenly realised, must run almost to the cliff edge, because the grass ended where the blue sky began and although she couldn't glimpse the waves she could hear their slow sigh and the grating of pebbles flung up the beach. A few gulls were circling, giving their harsh, melancholy cry before disappearing to dive downwards, the sun striking the underside of their arched white wings.

She started as the front door banged. A second later, Sam strode into the kitchen, his brows raggedly frowning.

'Couldn't he fix it?' she asked, alarmed by that stare.

'Oh, yes,' he said, halting in front of her, an odd undertone to his voice. 'It was quite simple once he'd located what was wrong.' His eyes pinned her like a moth on cardboard and she stiffened, wondering what was wrong now. 'Tell me, do you have a car?'

'Yes,' she said slowly. 'But I got the train to London, you see, or . . .'

'Know much about engines?' he interrupted.

'Not really,' she said ruefully. 'I can drive the thing but I take it to a garage if it goes wrong, unless one of my brothers is at home and can fix whatever's happened.'

'Such big, innocent eyes,' Sam said bitterly.

'And so plausible—my God, you almost convinced me and I know damned well you're lying. What was the big idea? Make sure you couldn't get away and had to stay the night? And then what? Was Draycott going to burst in here and accuse me of seducing you?' He stopped, his eyes narrowing. 'No, of course not—it was you who tipped Denise off about this place, wasn't it? You didn't need to stow away in my car—you already knew the address and you gave it to her yesterday. You weren't just an opportunist; your blackmail plan was made well in advance—that was the whole idea, wasn't it? That Denise should arrive and catch us alone here and I'd have to promise to give Draycott his job back in return for being let off the hook with Denise!'

Annabel was dumbfounded, staring at him with her mouth open. When she got her breath back she said mildly enough, 'You're crazy!'

'I must be,' he raged, his hands clenched at his sides. He lifted them towards her throat then snatched them down, snarling. 'No, last time I touched you I got myself into even more trouble— I'm not making that mistake again! I thought you were simply a well-meaning nuisance, but you're much more dangerous than that, aren't you? You're a scheming, cold-blooded little . . .'

'Hey!' Annabel broke in before he could finish that sentence. She didn't think she would like whatever he had been about to call her. 'I don't know what you're talking about, but . . .'

'Oh, no, of course you don't,' he sneered, his eyes becoming insolent as they slid over her. Annabel began to feel really nervous—why was he looking at her like that? What had happened to make Sam change into a hostile stranger again?

'You were taking a bit of a risk, weren't you?' he asked insultingly. 'What if I'd been less than gentlemanly last night? You might have had to put up with more than just a night on the couch in the sitting room—or were you prepared to do literally anything to get Draycott his job back?'

Bewildered, she watched him uneasily. His face had the taut symmetry of some African carving, cheekbones sharp and angular under skin whose texture the sunlight picked out for her, mouth brooding, a little cruel and the jawline rigid with what she could see was a desire to hit her.

'Did he know what you planned? Was he ready to let you spend the night with me just to get his job back?' Sam asked, his mouth distasteful.

'Will you tell me what this is all about?' she demanded, struggling to keep her cool under that menacing stare. She was frightened by him, but she didn't want Sam Jerrard to know that. 'What are you accusing me of?' she added when he just stared at her, his mouth wry.

'Very well, go on playing the innocent,' he retorted. 'But you know what I'm talking about— when the mechanic began checking over my car he did what I should have done right away. He took off the distributor head and of course he saw at once that the rotor arm was missing.

She stared blankly. 'What's a rotor arm?'

Sam said something that made her blench. Nobody had ever called her that before. Turning on his heel he walked across the room and then back again in a tense, loping prowl, as though trying to control his rage. Annabel watched him apprehensively as he confronted her again; his nostrils pinched, his eyes narrow, his mouth set.

After a brief silence he said succinctly, 'There's no point in lying.'

'I'm not . . .'

'God in heaven,' he burst out, then took a deep breath. 'Miss Walsh, once I found out that that rotor arm had gone I knew it had to be sabotage—it couldn't have simply fallen out, you know. Somebody had to open the distributor and take it out. Who else could have done it? You're the only possible suspect.'

Confused and bewildered, Annabel didn't say anything when he paused, and was given a cold smile.

'It was brilliantly thought out and executed—clever stuff, Miss Walsh. Beautiful economy, too. Nothing could have been simpler, could it? You waited until I was asleep and then you slipped out, took off the distributor head and removed the rotor arm. What did you do with it, by the way? Chuck it over the hedge into the long grass? Anyway, two minutes later you were back indoors and curled up on the couch looking as if butter wouldn't melt in your mouth,' He eyed her consideringly. 'I suppose you were wide awake when I came along to wake you up this morning, the first time? You had me fooled, lying there with the blankets kicked off, looking like a sleeping angel.'

Her eyes flickered nervously at that picture of herself with him watching her and Sam laughed angrily.

'Was that another little trap set for me? Was I supposed to be tempted to stay with you?' He watched the crimson flow of colour through her face without compunction. 'Well, I almost fell for it,' he bit out. 'I was fool enough to hesitate before I went out again and I was an ever bigger fool than that—I hated myself for thinking what I did when I saw you lying there. I wasn't even that annoyed when I couldn't start the car. I half admired you for being so loyal to Draycott and going to such lengths to save his job—but then I didn't know just how far you would go, did I?'

She backed away from the force of that last question and his mouth tightened, twisting bitterly.

'No, don't worry—I'm not going to hit you, much as I'd like to right now. Nothing on this earth would get me to come within an inch of you after this—you're far too dangerous, Miss Walsh. As soon as the mechanic gets back with a new rotor arm I'll drive you home, all the way home. Until then, stay out of my sight.'

He walked away, slamming the door behind him, and Annabel sat down weakly on the nearest chair, her legs trembling. She couldn't think straight for a moment or two, her mind dazed and muddled, but then one question shot into her head. She knew she hadn't taken this rotor arm out of Sam's car, but if she hadn't who had?

CHAPTER FIVE

HALF an hour later, they drove away from the
cottage in a brooding silence, which Annabel
hesitantly broke as she saw that they were
approaching the outskirts of a small village some
miles later. Giving his averted profile a quick
glance she began: 'You can drop me here if . . .'

'I'm taking you to your front door,' Sam Jerrard
informed her curtly. 'I want to make sure I've seen
the last of you.'

She sank into silence again, staring out of the
side window, watching the flat countryside flash
by. What did he intend to do about Charlie? she
wondered miserably. Her intervention hadn't done
Charlie's cause much good, had it? It would have
been much better if she hadn't tried to help, but
her intentions had been good; it wasn't her fault
that everything had gone wrong.

Who had taken that rotor arm? Her brows knit
as she thought back over the events of the previous
day. She and Sam had been quite alone at the
cottage and nobody had known that they were
there.

Except Gwen, of course. Her eyes opened wider.
Could Gwen be behind all this? But then that
would mean that Gwen had followed them down
here, sneaked into the garage, taken the rotor arm
and crept away.

She shifted impatiently, scowling. No, it was

absurd. A stupid idea—why should Gwen do it? What possible motive could she have?

Sam Jerrard drove fast; too fast, in Annabel's opinion, spinning around corners and churning up mud on the low-lying roads they took across country, his tyres hissing on the puddles they frequently encountered. She gave him an apprehensive look but didn't dare to say anything. He was staring ahead, his profile a series of sharp angles, that long lean body taut under the black sweater and black cords he wore. Just that one look at him warned her to hold her tongue. It was some slight reassurance to see how easily his powerful hands controlled the wheel, but Annabel still hated driving at that speed.

He suddenly turned his head, shot her a hard stare. 'Well?'

'Well what?' she asked, uncertainly.

'You were going to say something?'

'Was I?'

'Don't fence with me, Miss Walsh. Out with it.' He laughed without humour. 'I imagine I can guess what's on your mind, though. You want to know what I'm going to do about Draycott now, don't you?'

She took a deep breath. 'I suppose I . . .'

'Yes, I thought so. I'm beginning to read you like a book.' There was a gritty satisfaction in the way he said that; his smile could have curdled milk. He took another corner and she held on to her seat, convinced they were driving on two wheels.

'This isn't Brands Hatch,' she gasped.

He ignored that. 'Well, I haven't made up my

mind yet, frankly. My first reaction was to decide
that Draycott would get his job back over my dead
body and that you could join him in the
unemployment queue, but that was before I'd
realised that you had got me over a barrel. Oh, I
know you haven't pointed that out to me yet, but I
suppose you're waiting for me to cool down before
you close in for the kill.'

She watched him intently—now what, she
wondered? Was this what he had been brooding
about while he drove like a fiend out of hell?

He threw her another glittering look; his eyes
had the savage brilliance of ice in sunshine. 'Oh,
come on, Miss Walsh—we both know what comes
next, don't we? I was a bit slow on the uptake, you
see. I thought, when I found out about the car,
that that spiked your little game, but of course we
were only in round one, weren't we? You knew
that as soon as I discovered the rotor arm was
missing I'd guess you'd taken it—but that didn't
bother you, did it? Because I was still caught in
your trap. If I sack Draycott, you'll make sure
Denise hears that you spent the night at my
cottage with me.' His hand crashed down on the
wheel of the car, the car swerved violently and
Annabel gave a stifled cry of shock. 'My God,
you'll even be able to repeat to her all the things
she said in the bedroom ... tell her where you
were hiding ...' Sam's face worked convulsively in
the grip of blind rage. 'I ought to strangle you!'

She shrank back in her seat and he watched her,
a stain of red along his cheekbones, before
laughing with derisive bitterness.

'No, don't worry—I've no intention of doing

anything so stupid. I've got enough problems because of you.'

A lorry thundered around the next corner and Annabel gave a terrified gasp. 'Watch the road!'

Sam missed the lorry by inches and the blare of the driver's horn followed them on their way. The shock made Sam lapse into that grim silence once more; he said nothing at all until they were almost at Blackstone.

On the outskirts of the little country town, he suddenly began to talk again in a calmer voice. 'I might as well face facts, I suppose. I have little choice, do I? We'll strike a bargain, Miss Walsh—from now on you will leave the talking to myself and Draycott. Yes, he can stay on at the lab but I want him to take two weeks off until I get back from Brussels. I'm flying there tomorrow and I can't back out of it. This business must wait until I get back. You had the idea that Draycott could continue with the theoretical side of the research while someone else did the practical work. That might be the wisest solution, but first I'll have to discuss the project with Draucott before I'm sure your idea is feasible.' He turned into the wide tree-lined avenue where Annabel lived. 'This is it, isn't it?' he said, slowing as he approached the gate of her house.

'How did you know?' she asked, puzzled.

'I used to live in Blackstone myself, remember? I know the town like the back of my hand.' He braked and sat with both hands on the wheel staring up at the pleasant semi-detached house. A willow grew in the garden, obscuring some of the windows, the branches just beginning to put out leaves around the fluffy yellow catkins, which showered the sunny air with a cloud of delicate, floating golden dust. 'Quite idyllic,' Sam Jerrard said sarcastically.

Annabel summoned up all her courage; he seemed less violent now. 'Look, I didn't take the rotor arm out of your car,' she began and he turned on her.

'Who did then?'

'I don't know—it wasn't me, that's all; I don't know a rotor arm from a sparking plug.' She looked anxiously at his unyielding face. 'Honestly, Mr Jerrard, I didn't do it.'

'Who else would have a motive?' he asked unanswerably and she slowly shook her head.

'Was it Draycott?' he asked, watching her.

'Of course not—Charlie didn't even know where I was—I didn't have time to let him know what I meant to do. He knew I'd gone to London to see you but . . .'

'He asked you to talk to me?' She saw his mouth indent impatiently, with unhidden contempt. Sam Jerrard despised Charlie for that, she realised—he was a very different type of man; he'd never ask a woman to intervene on his behalf.

Defensively, she said, 'Charlie isn't very good with words, he can't talk to people.'

'But he let you go to London to save his neck? Don't tell me it didn't occur to him that I might want something in exchange.' He looked down at her, his eyes mocking, the dark pupils glowing and holding her uneasy gaze. 'I'm beginning to think I was a fool not to strike a bargain with you last night—that was obviously what you expected, in spite of your vague talk about ringing Draycott to come and bring you home. Those big green eyes of your look so innocent it didn't dawn on me that you were waiting for me to suggest a quid pro quo.'

Annabel opened the door and almost fell out in her haste. From the safety of the pavement she said furiously, 'For the last time, I wasn't expecting anything of the kind, I didn't take anything out of your car and I wasn't blackmailing you.' She didn't wait for an answer, but turned and walked up the short drive to her house, fighting her way through the drooping willow branches which tangled with her hair and clutched at her like bony fingers.

Sam Jerrard called after her: 'Tell Draycott I'll see him in two weeks' time. He isn't to go near the laboratories until I get back.'

As she reached the front door, Annabel heard Sam Jerrard drive away, but she hesitated before letting herself into the house. How was she going to explain to her parents that she had come home early from her weekend in London without having bought the wedding outfit she had supposedly gone to buy, and without the suitcase she had taken with her?

She had deposited that in a left luggage office at the mainline railway station when she first arrived in London. She had intended to pick it up again when she had seen Sam Jerrard. The station was only ten minutes by taxi from her brother Joe's flat, where her mother had arranged for her to spend the weekend.

Annabel knew that by now Joe or his wife,

Sandra, would have rung Mr and Mrs Walsh to ask why Annabel hadn't shown up, and this first indication that something had happened to their only daughter would have sent shock waves through the family. Her mother was given to free-wheeling bouts of imagination—the very fact that she preferred to dream about travelling to exotic places while staying cheerfully close to home meant that Elaine Walsh's taste for melodrama had more scope. She wasn't hampered by the reality of places. They existed in her mind in a technicolour heightening which visiting them might have destroyed. To Elaine Walsh, London was a confusing, bewildering, wicked city whose streets were lawless after dark, and ever since she realised that Annabel was lost in that dangerous maze, she would have been beside herself.

Taking a deep breath, Annabel found her key and put it into the lock, but at that second the front door opened abruptly and her brother Patrick eyed her quizzically.

'Where on earth have you been? Charlie and I were just wondering how to break the news to Mum and Dad that you'd vanished off the face of the earth!'

Annabel peered past him, flapping her hands. 'Ssh . . . where are they?'

'They'll be eating sandwiches by now,' Patrick pronounced, consulting his watch. 'And Mum will be feeding her crusts to the ducks while Dad takes his wellies off to wriggle his toes.'

Annabel sagged in relief. 'They've gone fishing?'

'All day,' her brother nodded, grinning at her. 'And before you ask—no, they don't know you didn't spend the night at Joe's. He rang here at eleven o'clock last night to ask where the hell you were, and did you think his place was a hotel . . . I took the call; Mum and Dad were already fast asleep—you know how early they go to bed when they're going fishing next day.' Patrick let her walk past him.

'And you didn't tell them?' she asked, turning to watch him shut the front door.

'I wasn't up when they left—I'd have had to tell them when they got back, though. They'd have hung, drawn and quartered me if I'd kept my mouth shut any longer.' Patrick's rugged face held a glimmer of rueful amusement. 'And to tell the truth, Annie old darling, I was beginning to get the tiniest bit worried about you.' He pulled her through the hall and pushed her into the kitchen where Charlie was making mugs of instant soup.

He looked round, his eyes boggling in his head. 'Annabel!'

'No need to make it sound as if I'm the monster from the great pit,' Annabel said crossly, throwing herself on to a chair.

'I'm so glad to see you,' Charlie said with fervour.

'It sounded more like horror. Can I have one of those mugs of soup? I'm starving.' The memory of Sam Jerrard's excellent breakfast reproached her, but she had been through a good deal since the mushrooms, bacon and tomatoes. She felt she had used up all their energy value.

Her loving brother grabbed one of the mugs quickly and slunk off with it to a chair by the window. 'This is mine. Make her another one, Charlie.'

Charlie looked wistfully at the soup, then handed his to Annabel with a self-sacrificing smile. 'Here, take this—I'll make myself another one,' he said, then stood gazing down at her as she began to sip the tomato concoction in the mug. 'Oh, Annabel, thank heavens you're back! I was beginning to think . . .'

'We thought Sam Jerrard might have carried you off into white slavery,' Patrick said cheerfully.

'The idea doesn't seem to have turned your hair grey,' Annabel retorted with bitterness.

'I was very worried,' Charlie protested.

'I was sorry for Sam Jerrard,' Patrick said. 'I know you better than Charlie does—I wondered how you'd do it.'

'Do what?' Annabel gasped, almost dropping her mug.

'Kill him.' Patrick had glee in his voice; he liked making people jump. He closely resembled Annabel at a casual glance—his hair was reddish and his eyes a hazel green. Of course, he was built in a very different way—nature's design having been improved by years of playing rugger, cricket, squash and any other game known to the local males. Patrick was muscled and fit and highly desirable, according to Annabel's girl-friends who had been queuing up to go out with him ever since Annabel started school at the age of five and found herself very popular as Patrick's little sister. She couldn't understand it, herself. She knew Patrick too well—he had no mystery for her and no magic, and Patrick's lazy grin now made it clear that Annabel had no mystery for him, either.

Annabel looked from her brother to Charlie

indignantly. 'Well, you two are really something! You thought I might have been carried off by Sam Jerrard but you didn't do a thing to save me? I'd hate to have to rely on you two for help in a tight situation.'

Patrick finished his soup and leaned back, his feet on the window-sill and his body lazily stretched out. 'We knew you could handle it, kid. These are the days of female liberation and, anyway, we taught you how to punch and where to hit so it really hurt, didn't we? You can't say we didn't give you a good basic training in self-defence.'

'I ought to hit *you* where it hurts,' threatened Annabel, glowering, and Patrick warily folded up in case she meant it.

Charlie drew up a chair and looked soberly at her. 'What did happen? Where have you been?'

'I've been with Sam Jerrard all night,' Annabel told him maliciously, just to see his eyes bulge, as they did, in horrified silence.

Patrick sat up, too. 'Hey, you're kidding,' he said, then on another breath, 'Aren't you?'

'No.' The uncompromising monosyllable made the two men look at each other, mouths open but wordless.

'What happened, kid?' Patrick asked with a new tenderness, getting up and coming over to squat down at eye level, taking her hands. He and Annabel were very close. They had an easy-going relationship which was never sentimental, and in which Charlie had always been a third.

Annabel slapped his hands away, glaring at him. 'Not what you're thinking!'

She saw relief flash through her brother's face, then he got up, resuming his lazy amusement; but Charlie was less easy to reassure.

'What did he do, the swine? If he laid a hand on you, I'll pulverise him and I don't care if he does give my project to someone else. I wouldn't work for him again for a million pounds!' He was very red and breathing like a winded horse.

Relenting, Annabel told him to stop worrying. 'I slept in his sitting room on a couch.' She went on to give them the whole story to which they listened with fascination.

It was Patrick who put his finger on the nub of the problem. 'But if you didn't snitch his rotor arm, who did? You don't think he did it himself, as some sort of revenge? So that he could threaten you . . .' Patrick broke off, grimacing. 'No, not very likely, is it? I mean, if he'd done it the night before—to keep you at the cottage all night, I could understand it.'

'Oh, could you,' muttered Annabel. 'What a lovely mind you've got. That's what you'd have done, I suppose?'

'Well, it would be a good wheeze—I must remember it if ever I want to persuade a girl to stay the night.' Her brother grinned at her. She didn't grin back, but eyed him with disgust.

'You treacherous worm, I ought to warn your girlfriends about that mind of yours.'

Charlie was looking hopeful. 'But he definitely said I could have my job back? Is he likely to turn nasty with me over this, though? I mean, now he knows I asked you to talk to him—he may blame me for the whole thing.'

'No,' Annabel said with a sigh. 'He blames me.'
There was a little silence.

'I bet it was Gwen Bridge,' Charlie said
suddenly. 'Everyone says she's very possessive
about Jerrard; she's been working for him almost
since the beginning. She isn't married, either. I've
heard that she's been in love with him for years
but he's never noticed.'

'Is she pretty?' asked Patrick with a spark of
interest.

Charlie made a face. 'Thin and tart, like a green
apple.'

'It doesn't make sense,' Annabel told them both.
'If she was in love with him, why would she want
to strand me at his cottage alone with him?'

Patrick thought that over. 'So that this fiancée
could find you there?'

Annabel stared, frowning.

'And break off the engagement,' Charlie added,
nodding vigorously. 'Now that makes sense,
doesn't it, Annabel?'

She had to admit it did. 'I've a good mind to go
up to London and face her with it,' she said,
bristling. 'I think you're right—after all, nobody
else knew I'd be there.'

'I shouldn't,' said Patrick. 'Leave it alone now,
kid. Charlie's got his job back and you're well out
of it. From now on, I'd stay out of Jerrard's way,
if I were you.'

'I've every intention of staying out of his way. I
hope I never see him again,' Annabel said, getting
up. Sam Jerrard had made it plain that he never
wanted to see her again, so they should have no
problem. She could go further—she wished she

had never set eyes on him at all. A man like that should be labelled with a government health warning—this man is dangerous to your health, he can seriously damage your peace of mind. Just remembering the way he had kissed her made her head feel heavy and languorous, as though she had been drugged.

'I'm going up to change, then I'm going shopping,' she told Patrick and Charlie. 'I'd better have some new clothes to show Mum or she'll get suspicious. Oh, by the way—Patrick, will you ring Joe and warn him not to say a word to Mum and Dad about me not turning up at his place last night?'

Patrick nodded. 'Can I tell him why you went missing? He's bound to ask.'

'Tell him I stayed with a friend.'

Her brother's gaze was cynical. 'Joe's interpretation of that excuse will be pretty hair-raising.'

'Oh, tell him what you like then,' Annabel fumed, making for the door. 'And don't embroider the story, the truth is bad enough.'

Charlie pursued her into the hall. 'Annabel, I'm very grateful . . . I don't know how to thank you.'

'Don't blow the lab up again, that'll be gratitude enough,' she said with a sharpness which made him wince.

'I hope it wasn't too much of an ordeal—I'd never have asked you to talk to Sam Jerrard if I'd thought something like that would happen. It was marvellous of you to go to so much trouble, but you shouldn't have hidden in his car, you know, I'd never have let you do it if I'd known.'

'What's all this stuff about you not letting me

do this or that? I'm not your property, Charlie Draycott. I don't have to ask you for permission to do anything.' She put her foot on the first stair, looking back over her shoulder. 'But you can take me out to dinner somewhere really swish—you owe me a good dinner and I'd rather be out tonight when Mum and Dad get back; it will save a lot of awkward questions. I'll get back very late and tell them I decided not to stay in London over Sunday. They'll think I caught the last train back.'

Charlie looked unhappy. 'I don't like the idea of lying to your parents.'

'What Mum doesn't know, she can't grieve over,' Annabel told him ruthlessly. 'If she does ever find out I was alone with Sam Jerrard in that cottage all night she'll make us both wish we'd never been born. Are you ready to face her when she's in one of her Grand Inquisitor moods?'

Charlie backed, horrified, and she nodded at him.

'Exactly. I thought you'd rather lie. This is where discretion is definitely the better part of valour. Nothing happened that I'm ashamed of, but my mother wouldn't believe that until she'd had an account of every single second I spent under that roof, and even then I'd never hear the end of it. She would babble on about the risk I'd run until I went deaf.'

'Mothers are like that,' Charlie agreed gloomily, obviously thinking about his own. Mrs Draycott was a widow and Charlie was her only child. He wasn't so much tied to her apron strings as bound hand and foot to them. Mrs Draycott was a nice woman and Annabel had got on well with her during the years when she, Patrick and Charlie were growing up but, Mrs Draycott was no longer so welcoming. She was terrified of Charlie getting married and leaving home. He was her whole life and she was a shy, nervous woman with few friends. Once her son had gone Mrs Draycott foresaw a lonely life in front of her.

Annabel went up to her room and changed into a white sweater and jeans. When she came down again Patrick had left and Charlie was waiting for her.

'I'll pick you up at six, then,' he said. 'We'll drive out to The Three Jolly Bargemen for dinner. Will that suit you?'

'Fabulous,' Annabel enthused. The large country inn had a very high reputation in Norfolk—they offered first-class food served with style and elegance. 'You'd better book or we might not get a table, especially on a Saturday night,' she pointed out and Charlie grinned complacently.

'I booked while you were getting changed—they said it was the last table in the place, so now they're fully booked. Lucky I thought of it.'

Annabel slid into her jacket and opened the door. 'I'll have lunch out and get my shopping done. If I haven't got something spectacular to wear at Andy's wedding my mother will want to know why. I think I'll drive into Norwich. I've already exhausted the shops in Blackstone, and, anyway, my mother will know where I got it if I turn up with something from here.'

She got into her car under Charlie's eyes, wound the window down and leaned out. 'Don't be late—six o'clock sharp. Mum and Dad will get back at around seven, if I know them. Dad won't stop fishing until it's dark and it will take them half an hour to drive home. I think six o'clock is safe enough.' She started the engine and drove away, leaving Charlie standing on the pavement staring after her. The sun turned his buttery curls to gold and he looked very handsome in his grey flannel trousers and lemon sweater. In her driving mirror Annabel saw several girls walk past, eyeing him sideways. Charlie was unaware of them, his mind on other things. Poor Charlie, she thought, making a face. He didn't really know he was alive.

It was unfair to compare him with Sam Jerrard, but she couldn't help doing it. In some ways, Charlie was much more handsome, but he simply didn't do anything to her pulse rate, whereas Sam Jerrard's impact on her had been little short of catastrophic. She didn't think she'd ever be the same again. Not that she liked him, of course. Far from it. He was too much the dominant male. Annabel wasn't putting up with his particular brand of macho domination and she was glad she'd been more or less warned to stay out of his way in future. She wouldn't need telling twice, she thought defiantly.

By the time she reached Norwich it was really too late to get lunch so she made do with a hamburger and coffee before she began to hunt through the shops for something to wear for her brother Andy's wedding. As it was Saturday afternoon, the city was crowded, but eventually Annabel found a dress she liked: a smooth lemon jersey wool with a delightful ruff-like white pleated collar of silk and a chic little matching jacket

which was cut off just above the waist. She
managed to get shoes and a handbag in a very
attractive diamond design, yellow and white,
which perfectly accompanied the dress and jacket,
and as an afterthought bought a small white
bowler hat with a white veil which would half hide
her eyes.

Annabel hated wearing hats, but she knew that
that would please her mother and distract Elaine
Walsh from probing too deeply into what Annabel
had been doing in London. Elaine Walsh had a
passion for hats; she thought they were feminine
and elegant, and was grieved by Annabel's
reluctance to wear them.

By the time Annabel had loaded her packages
into the boot of her car it was still only four
o'clock so she went for a stroll through Norwich's
narrow streets. The city had been a centre of the
medieval wool trade and was full of fascinating old
houses and churches, their white and black timber
creaking in the spring wind, as if they were
moored galleys. Every time Annabel turned a
corner she caught another glimpse of the tapering
spire of the city's Norman cathedral, which she
had often visited in the past. Before driving home
she had tea in a small tea shop, enjoying the home-
made scones and jam and cream, the tiny
triangular sandwiches and the pot of strong
fragrant tea, the more because she had eaten so
little since that breakfast at Sam Jerrard's cottage.

When she got home, she was relieved to find her
parents hadn't yet returned and as she and Charlie
left for dinner in the pale mothy dusk there was
still no sign of Mr and Mrs Walsh. 'Perhaps

they're stopping for dinner somewhere,' Annabel thought aloud, then made a face. 'I hope they don't turn up at The Three Jolly Bargemen.'

Charlie looked petrified. 'So do I.'

'You make a rotten conspirator,' Annabel said derisively. 'Stop your teeth chattering and keep your mind on the road. Even if they are there, they can't eat us.' She began to giggle. 'The management would probably tell them customers weren't allowed to bring their own food.'

'That isn't funny,' Charlie said gloomily, and looked around with some trepidation as he turned into the large car park of the country inn. A number of other cars were already parked there, but Charlie quicky realised that the Walsh car wasn't among them, and began to relax. It was Annabel who had the traumatic shock as she was getting out of his car and suddenly noticed a big white Rolls parked in splendid isolation right at the far side of the car park.

She stiffened, staring. She hadn't taken Denise Keiron's number but she had a sinking suspicion that it was the same car. Hard on the heels of that thought came another. Surely Sam Jerrard wasn't going to be here too?

'Oh, no,' she moaned to herself and Charlie spun round from locking his car.

'What's up?' He looked around furtively. 'You haven't spotted your parents, have you?'

'No,' Annabel said wildly. 'But if that Rolls belongs to Denise Keiron we might find ourselves eating cheek by jowl with Sam Jerrard.' She caught hold of Charlie as he dived back to his car and began to unlock it again. 'Don't be such a cowardy custard! If he's with his fiancée, he won't come over and beat you up.'

She had to drag Charlie into the restaurant, his heels churning gravel at every step. The head waiter gave him a narrow-eyed stare, not surprisingly as Charlie was giving a good imitation of a man on the run, sinking his chin into his shirt collar, trying to look invisible. 'Draycott, sir?' The head waiter consulted his book. 'Hmm . . .' He looked up, reluctantly admitting that they had a reservation, and swept them through the spacious room. Annabel carefully did not look around. If Sam Jerrard was here, she didn't want to see him. With any luck she would find herself with her back to his table.

The head waiter left them and they ordered an aperitif, a Kir for Annabel and a gin and tonic for Charlie, who looked as though he needed it, lifting the glass to his lips and swallowing half the contents while he stared desperately around him.

'Oh, God,' he whispered, almost spilling the other half of the drink. 'You were right. They are here. Behind you, half way down the room, behind that third pillar. I don't think they've seen us.'

Annabel stared at her menu, refusing to look up. 'Don't look at them,' she commanded under cover of reading the list of soups. 'Potage créole, I wonder what that is? Sounds delicious.'

'He's facing us, unluckily,' Charlie groaned, hiding behind his own menu.

'Ignore them,' Annabel said. 'I'm ravenous—I think I'll have beef stroganoff, they serve it with gorgeous saffron rice here.'

'He can't make a scene here, can he?' Charlie pleaded, ducking his head across the table.

'Of course he can't and, anyway, while he's with her he won't dare breath a word about last night. In fact, I'm ready to bet he's going to pretend he hasn't noticed us, and she won't recognise us, either. I don't suppose we made any impact on her. She doesn't notice anyone she thinks is beneath her level and we're definitely that.'

Their waiter returned to take their order and Annabel sipped her cool Kir, enjoying its delicious flavour without haste, while she told Charlie about the clothes she had bought that day.

'Andy's lucky to be marrying Kay, she's going to be a great sister-in-law. I prefer her to Sandra, there's something a little too career woman about Sandra—of course, she and Joe need the money so she has to work, but I often get the impression that she's much more interested in her job than she is in Joe. She's too hard-boiled and she hasn't any sense of humour these days. Perhaps she's working too hard to have time to have fun, but it's tough on Joe; he can't compete and I get the feeling he doesn't see much of her even at weekends.'

Charlie nodded as he began eating the smoked mackerel paté he had ordered. 'Patrick said much the same thing to me this morning.'

'He and Joe were good friends but we don't see much of Joe lately. Sandra doesn't like driving to Norfolk too often, I think. She prefers London.'

'Well, that's one thing about Kay—she hates cities. She's a nice girl, she'll suit Andy to the ground.'

Andrew Walsh was a surveyor working with the

local council and his future wife worked for them, too, in the rates department, but Kay had already admitted that as soon as she and Andy could afford it she was going to have a baby and give up work. That would not be for quite a while, as they wanted to have their own home first, and Kay's salary would be an essential part of their budget for at least a couple of years.

They were half-way through their main course when Annabel heard a faint stir among the other diners and looked up to see Denise Keiron walking across the room. Ruefully, Annabel noted the smart black and gold dress she wore—every time she saw the blonde girl Denise was wearing something different. How much did she spend on clothes? wondered Annabel, unable to suppress a faint envy. Her own budget restricted the amount she spent on clothes, but she got by because she wore jeans and T-shirts a good deal of the time.

Denise vanished into the powder room. Annabel let her eyes drift vaguely across the other tables towards where Sam Jerrard sat. He had a glass of brandy in one hand and was staring into it as her gaze reached him, but a second later he glanced up and she found herself looking straight into those cool, grey eyes. A fever started, deep inside her, her body burning with awareness and a strange sort of anger with him. He was tough enough with Charlie and with herself—he laid down the law to everyone who worked for him, enforced his own will ruthlessly, and was quick enough to resent anyone who disobeyed or annoyed him—and yet he was weak with Denise, danced to her tune, let her wind him around her little finger and was so scared of her reaction if she found out that he had had another girl at the cottage, that he was prepared to submit to blackmail.

Her stare became contemptuous, her mouth hardened. Sam's eyes narrowed, reading her face immediately, his black brows jerking together. Annabel looked away.

It was stupid to be surprised by Sam's weakness with Denise. Hadn't her brothers shown her that men were always weak with girls like Denise Keiron? Sex was as volatile an ingredient as anything Charlie used in his experiments—and sex was what Denise Keiron flaunted from her blonde head down to her long, shapely legs.

'You're very quiet,' Charlie said tentatively, his hand reaching across the table to attract her attention, then he flinched visibly as Annabel turned furious green eyes on him. 'What's the matter?'

'Men make me sick,' Annabel ground out. 'You're all so stupid, women can run rings round you.' Then she relented, seeing Charlie's astounded, bewildered expression, and grimaced, patting his hand. 'Never mind, you can't help it,' she reassured. 'I don't know who invented sex but the experiment was an abysmal failure.'

Charlie stared at her uncertainly. 'I'm very grateful to you for saving my job, Annabel.' He looked around, pink to his hairline, then muttered without meeting her eyes: 'I've been meaning to ask ... well, what I ... do you think we might ... well, not right away, but sometime would you ...'

'What?' she prompted, wondering what on earth

was in his mind now. If he was going to ask her to talk to Sam Jerrard for him again he could save his breath. As far as she was concerned Sam Jerrard did not exist; she would die rather than go anywhere near him.

'Marry me?' Charlie ended with a gulp.

CHAPTER SIX

CHARLIE dropped Annabel outside her home just before midnight. He was in a very cheerful mood—euphoric, she thought drily, reading the expression of his eyes as she said good night and got back a broad grin. Charlie had waited for her reaction to his proposal with all the apprehension of someone waiting for judgment on a hanging charge and when she gently said, 'Of course I'm very flattered, Charlie, nobody ever proposed to me before, but I don't feel I'm ready for marriage yet!' she had seen his eyes flood with relief and had struggled not to laugh out loud. She guessed that he had proposed because he felt he owed her something for having saved his job; she knew it wasn't because Charlie was in love with her. Oh, he was fond of her, the sort of fondness her brothers felt, but with one difference—that Charlie had been imbued from boyhood with a sense of chivalry towards women by his mother, who would certainly be aghast if she realised to what dangers she had exposed her darling son and heir by constantly stressing that he ought to treat women like porcelain, and be grateful to them for their care of him. Mrs Draycott had, of course, meant that Charlie should be grateful to herself, should treat *her* like porcelain. She hadn't meant Annabel and she wouldn't want Charlie to get married.

'Oh, well, some other time then,' Charlie had said in delighted confusion.

'Yes, I'll take a rain check,' Annabel had promised, biting her lip.

'I mean ... you are sure?' Charlie looked agonised. 'Aren't you?'

'Certain.'

'Because Patrick said ...' He went redder, and her eyes narrowed.

'What did Patrick say?'

'Oh, just that we see a lot of each other, he wondered if there was anything in it.' Charlie ran a finger round the inside of his collar.

'Oh, it was Patrick's idea that you should propose?' Wait until I see my brother, she thought vengefully, brooding; how dare he put ideas in poor Charlie's empty head? Patrick knows Charlie can't actually think for himself.

'And you went to so much trouble for me,' Charlie confided. 'Very decent of you, I felt ...'

'That you owed me marriage, at least?' prompted Annabel. He blinked like a rabbit caught in headlights, suspecting that he was in some sort of trouble, but by no means sure from which direction or why.

'I'm not putting this very well,' he said unhappily and she took pity on him, patting his hand.

'Never mind, Charlie. Take no notice of Patrick, he was pulling your leg.' She saw his face clear. He was used to having his leg pulled by Patrick, who had teased him since they were very small. Patrick was much quicker and cleverer than Charlie in almost all ways, even if Charlie was a brilliant scientist, or perhaps because of that. Charlie had neglected many aspects of life, while he concentrated with intense absorption on his one chosen area. He thought, lived, ate, drank and moved within narrow boundaries and everything outside chemistry was alien territory to him.

One day some woman would marry Charlie when he wasn't looking. It wouldn't be her. Annabel was fond of him but she did not want to marry him. All the same, Charlie was not the bachelor type, tied though he was to his mother's apron strings. He was too helpless and unwary, perfect husband material for the right sort of woman, and sooner or later he would be spotted and lassoed, and Annabel gleefully imagined the battle royal which would start then between Charlie's mother and his wife. Charlie's emotional myopia had one saving grace—he would scarcely be conscious of the war going on around him and over him: he would merely try to placate and please both sides and because he was a lovable idiot both women would hide the worst from him.

As she got out of the car that night Charlie said blithely: 'When I told Mother I'd been given a fortnight's leave she suggested I went down to Devon to stay with my Aunt Edna, did I tell you? We're leaving on Tuesday, so I'll see you when I get back, okay?'

Annabel laughed, eyeing him with comprehension. 'Okay, see you, Charlie.' She stood, watching him drive off, wondering if he was even vaguely aware that he was being snatched from the jaws of marital danger? Mrs Draycott didn't want Charlie hanging around Annabel with nothing on his mind—she was acting on the old theory that idle hands find mischief to do, no doubt. Annabel decided it was rather amusing to be seen in such a lurid light as a dangerous woman. Walking towards the house she swung her handbag, gazing through half-lowered lids in what she felt was a good imitation of a *femme fatale*.

Her pose was interrupted as the front door opened and Patrick leered out at her. 'Why are you pulling weird faces?' he enquired in brotherly frankness.

'Are the parents in bed?' hissed Annabel and he nodded.

'Hours ago.'

'Keep your voice down,' she said, pushing him back into the house. The door into the sitting room was open; she saw the lamp lit by the couch and on the small table a plate of sandwiches and a mug of cocoa, beside an open book. Patrick had settled down cosily to enjoy himself, obviously. Annabel walked into the room and picked up one of the sandwiches, peering at the filling. 'Mm . . . bacon, my favourite,' she said, taking a bite.

'Hey, that's mine—make your own,' Patrick said resentfully, trying to take the sandwich away.

She flung herself into a chair by the open fire which was cheerfully burning half-way up the chimney because Patrick had loaded several logs of apple wood on it. 'Listen, what do you mean by hinting to Charlie that he ought to get engaged to me soon?' she accused and Patrick started to laugh, leaning against the mantel-shelf with firelight playing across his face.

'He didn't propose?'

'He did,' she confirmed grimly. 'I don't know what he'd have done if I'd accepted him, poor lamb—gone home and cut his throat, I should think. I don't know which of us was most appalled by the idea.'

'I was only kidding!'

'I know that, but Charlie didn't. He never does know when you're taking a rise out of him.'

Patrick sat on the couch and finished his little supper while she told him about Charlie's relief at her refusal.

'He's an idiot,' Patrick said, stretching with a yawn. 'Oh, I told Mum and Dad that you came back early because London gave you a headache, and Mum said she wasn't surprised, it always gave her one. She asked if you'd got some new clothes to wear at Andy's wedding, and I said it hadn't even entered my head to ask and she said I was useless and went off to bed happy.'

'Thanks, Patrick,' Annabel said gratefully.

'Any time, kid,' he shrugged, yawning, then looked at the clock. 'I'm going to bed.'

Annabel cleared away his supper, put out the lights and followed him up the stairs a few minutes later. It wasn't until she was on the edge of sleep that Sam Jerrard slipped into her head again. Her eyes opened wide, she put her fingers on her lips, surprised to feel them burn and appalled to realise that she had been remembering the way he had kissed her early that morning. It seemed like a hundred years ago, so much had happened since, yet the memory was terrifyingly vivid.

She turned over, thumping her pillow and settled down again, hoping to evict all thought of

him from her head. She didn't want to think about
Sam Jerrard; she wished she could forget she had
ever set eyes on him.

During the next two weeks, her life was
comparatively peaceful but her brother Andy's
wedding meant, of course, the gathering of the
whole, scattered family for the occasion, and Mr
Walsh said wryly to his wife, 'I think we were wise
to have just one daughter, Elaine—thank heavens
the bride's family have to bear the brunt of
making all the arrangements.'

Mrs Walsh looked distinctly cross. 'I offered to
help Kay's mother, but she said she could
manage.'

'Oh, well, it *is* her big day!' Mr Walsh enjoyed
teasing his wife.

'Kay's the bride!' snapped Elaine Walsh.

'Kay's the excuse for all the excitement,' her
husband agreed, 'but it's Mrs Sumner who's been
waiting for this day for twenty years. I'm not
surprised she turned down your offer of help—
she's the centre of the stage and she isn't sharing
the limelight with anyone. But don't worry,
Elaine—your time will come. Annabel, how can
you keep your mother waiting like this? Surely
there's some young man you can marry?'

'Don't be silly, Philip!' scolded Mrs Walsh.

'Dad's just teasing you, Mum,' Annabel
soothed.

'I know that, I don't need you to tell me. Philip,
eat your egg before it gets cold.'

But Mrs Walsh gave Annabel a reproachful
glance at the same time, because under Mr Walsh's
teasing lay a certain truth. Mrs Walsh did dream

of Annabel's wedding day and had done so ever since she lay in bed with her new baby in her arms, looking ahead with dreamy eyes. Three of the Walsh boys were married now and Mrs Walsh had had to take a back seat at all their weddings while the bride's mother bustled about importantly, making decisions and giving orders. Elaine Walsh felt that Annabel wasn't trying. After all, she was twenty-three now. How much longer was she going to keep them waiting?

Annabel looked away, reading her mother's thoughts impatiently and with resentment. At nineteen she had wanted to get married soon. She had watched some of her friends marrying early and felt left out, left behind, but gradually she had come to feel that she wasn't ready for the responsibility and pressures of marriage. She enjoyed her job and she was a free agent; she could do what she liked. She didn't need marriage, it would only narrow her horizons.

After Charlie joined the firm, Annabel's horizons narrowed anyway, because he was never far from her side and people got the wrong impression. Other men got the wrong impression. They assumed that Charlie had rights over her, and Annabel could hardly hang out a sign saying: 'I am not Charlie Draycott's property.' She was trapped between her fondness for Charlie, and her reluctance to let him monopolise her. Charlie wasn't in love with her, any more than she was in love with Charlie—but how could she make that clear to the rest of the world without hurting him?

The wedding day was bright and clear, an April day without flaw. The bride's lace and silk gown was intensely romantic and her train of small bridesmaids in coral pink made everyone smile. The ceremony went off without a hitch and the bride's mother was even more radiant than the bride, while Mrs Walsh cried happily at the sight of her son looking unusually elegant in morning dress. Andy was more often seen in jeans; his wedding suit seemed to make him uneasy, he kept fidgeting with his grey silk tie and when Patrick grinned at him teasingly, he scowled back and offered to give his younger brother a kick if he said a word.

'It was a lovely wedding,' Annabel said to her sister-in-law, Sandra, during the reception. Sandra was not precisely her favourite person, but Annabel felt she had to be friendly with her for Joe's sake. Sandra certainly looked very elegant that afternoon, her dark hair swept up on top of her head and pinned there with a white ivory Spanish comb, her dark red dress giving her body a tigerish grace. Her expression spoilt the effect; Sandra always managed to give Annabel the impression that she was bored by the Walsh family and disdainful of her surroundings.

'When's your wedding?' Sandra asked without real interest. 'Joe introduced me to your young man, he's quite good-looking, isn't he?'

Annabel's teeth met. 'Charlie?' she muttered resentfully. 'I'm not marrying Charlie—I wish people would get the idea out of their heads.'

Sandra stared at her with lifted brows. 'No? Joe's convinced you're on the point of getting engaged to him, but then Joe is always getting the wrong end of the stick. I should have known better than to believe what *he* said.'

Annabel was taken aback by the bite in her sister-in-law's voice, doing a double take to stare at her. Before she could say anything, though, Charlie appeared to ask her to dance. He had got back from his holiday only the day before; Annabel hadn't had a chance to talk to him until now, but as they moved away she felt Sandra's cynical stare following them and flushed. No doubt Sandra was wondering if she had merely been protesting too much when she denied being about to get engaged to Charlie and that was the whole problem—while Charlie hovered around her all the time, nobody was going to believe that she wasn't in love with him.

'Good holiday?' she asked with stifled impatience as they danced to the disco beat being blared from the loudspeakers. Annabel found the strobe lighting disorientating. As it flashed around them it turned people's faces the oddest colour; everyone was suddenly a punk, even Mrs Draycott who was watching her son and Annabel dance with narrowed eyes. Her grey hair kept turning green and pink, which made Annabel giggle and look hurriedly away.

'The weather wasn't too good, but we managed to see quite a bit of the local scenery,' Charlie said without much excitement. 'I did get some fishing one day, but I had to drive Mum and Aunt Edna about most of the time.'

She eyed him pityingly. Poor Charlie, somebody ought to rescue him, but she had no intention of volunteering for the job, not any more. Some other brave lady could ride to his rescue in future. Annabel wasn't frightened of the dragons in

Charlie's life so much as afraid of being landed with Charlie permanently. She wondered thoughtfully about candidates for the post of Charlie's protector—several girls at the laboratory would be interested, but could they stand up to Mrs Draycott?

'Is Sam Jerrard back from Brussels yet?' Charlie asked and she stiffened, her body no longer flowing easily to the music.

'No idea,' she snapped, and Charlie looked surprised—he couldn't understand why Annabel was bristling like a cat that had had its fur stroked the wrong way.

'I thought you might have seen him,' he explained and she interrupted.

'Why should I have? What's Sam Jerrard to me?'

Charlie might have replied that Sam Jerrard was her boss, but he didn't; he simply looked confused and baffled, saying, 'Hasn't he been to the lab at all while I was away? I suppose he was serious, he will get in touch with me? You said he would, but I haven't heard a word from him.' His voice was reproachful as he stared at her and so were his eyes; Annabel wasn't proof against their helpless gaze.

Sighing, she soothed, 'He promised he'd see you as soon as he got back, so obviously he hasn't returned from Brussels yet. Don't worry, Charlie, it's going to be okay, he'll keep his word.' That was one thing she was certain about—Sam Jerrard was not a man who went back on his word.

The morning after the wedding, she slept until nearly eleven and got up to find the rest of the household in the same state of lethargic idleness. After a light breakfast they sat around reading the Sunday papers and exchanging the odd brief comment about both the news and yesterday's excitement. Mrs Walsh kept darting off to check on the Sunday lunch and while she was out of the room at one moment, Patrick said to his father, 'I'm worried about Joe, he seemed depressed.'

Mr Walsh looked up, his pipe between his teeth, nodding. 'Trouble between him and Sandra, do you think? Yes, I noticed that, too.'

'Noticed what?' asked Mrs Walsh, appearing like a genie from a bottle and immediately alert in case she had missed something.

Patrick looked at his father, allowing him to answer, and Mr Walsh gave his wife a rueful look. 'Joe didn't look too well,' he compromised.

'He looked worn out,' Mrs Walsh immediately leapt in ferociously. Joe, being the eldest, was her favourite son, just as Patrick, the youngest, was Mr Walsh's favourite, although each parent tried hard to hide their partiality, even from each other, and officially, at least, loved all their children equally. 'I suggested he and Sandra came here for a week. I think Joe needs a break, but of course *she* wouldn't have it! She said it was too cold up here. What did she expect in April? A heatwave?'

Annabel glanced at the window. The sky was grey and cloudy, now and then shot through with a shaft of pure gold from a sun in hiding. It was a typical spring day and a keen easterly wind was blowing across Norfolk's flat fields and weed-fringed water. Sandra was a town-bred girl; when she went on holiday she liked to bask in hot sunshine on a sandy beach. Annabel could understand why the tranquil country life they led up here was not exactly Sandra's idea of the perfect holiday, but Joe had grown up here, he loved Norfolk.

'Why don't you go up to town for a few days, Mum?' Patrick suggested. 'We'll be okay, Annabel's quite good with a can-opener and baked beans are very nutritious.'

Annabel threw a cushion at him and he grinned at her. Mr Walsh eyed his wife, who was knitting at full speed, her brow furrowed. 'What do you think, Elaine?' Mr Walsh asked warily.

'We could go if you like,' she said, refusing to commit herself.

'I think you should,' Patrick told them. 'Sandra's a weird girl—she seemed quite aggrieved because you and Dad hadn't visited them yet. That marriage is going through a bad patch, but you will be tactful, won't you?'

He received a furious, offended stare from his mother and a wry smile from his father. Annabel kicked him, grinning.

'Talking about tact,' she murmured, and Patrick laughed.

'Sorry, Mum.'

'So I should think!'

Mrs Walsh got up, folding her knitting and pushing it behind the cushion of her chair. 'I'm going to look at the lunch,' she said, leaving, and Annabel leaned back, eyes closing, listening to the wind in the trees and the comforting crackle of the fire.

Charlie appeared that afternoon, very on edge

as he waited to hear from Sam Jerrard. The wind had blown itself out and the rain had cleared; the sky was a tender, washed blue and sunlight picked out the daffodils and tulips in the garden and gave the willow leaves a new-minted clarity. Mr and Mrs Walsh had gone out to tea with friends. Patrick had a sudden rush of energy and suggested to Charlie that they should play golf. 'Want to come, Annabel? You can keep score for us,' they said.

'And carry your golf clubs, I suppose,' she said bitterly. 'No, thanks, I'm staying here. I'm going to wash my hair.'

'Women are so touchy these days,' Patrick said as she left the room. While Annabel was collecting her shampoo and a clean towel she heard the front door close behind them. It wasn't often she had the house to herself and she rather enjoyed the experience of being alone with nothing much to do.

She had just finished washing her hair and was about to towel it when she heard the front door bell ringing. Someone had a thumb on it, so she got the feeling it was urgent, and hurriedly wrapped the towel around her head into a turban and ran downstairs.

She had expected to see one or other of her brothers on the doorstep. They always rushed home if anything went wrong. It hadn't entered her head that it might be Sam Jerrard ringing at the door, and as she recognised him a wave of hot colour hit her face.

He watched her, frowning, harshness in the lines of that formidable jaw and mouth. 'I'm told

Draycott is here,' he said, as if it was some sort of accusation, biting out the words between those cold lips.

'Yes, he ...' Annabel began, so conscious of wearing nothing but a belted towelling robe that she couldn't meet his eyes, and had to look away, even more flushed and distinctly shaky. 'I mean, no, he isn't here at the moment,' she added, trying to pull herself together.

'No?' he queried, lifting one brow in icy disbelief.

Charlie was so worried about not hearing from Sam Jerrard, what a pity he had missed him by half an hour, Annabel thought. She could ring the golf club and tell Charlie to come back at once, of course.

'If you ... could come back in an hour?' she asked in a stammer. 'I think I could find him for you.'

'I'm sure you could,' he said and she glanced up then to find him running those arctic eyes over her from head to foot.

That was when she caught on to what was in his mind and Annabel stiffened with offence. He thought she had Charlie in the house, no doubt in her bedroom!

'He's playing golf with my brother,' she snapped. 'You could always go off to the golf course and find them or I'll ring and ask them to come back here.'

His expression changed slightly and she whipped the towel off her head, letting her wet red hair tumble down around her face, shaking it so that it sprayed Sam Jerrard with drops of scented water.

'I was washing my hair!' she told him furiously, stepping back to slam the door in his face.

Unfortunately, at the same instant Sam stepped forward, perhaps believing that she was inviting him in, and the door swung shut on his foot. Annabel heard his grunt of pain and, horrified, pulled the door open again. 'Oh, I'm so sorry!'

Sam hopped through it, clutching his foot, and sat down on a chair. 'You're almost as lethal as your boyfriend!' he muttered, massaging his toe.

Annabel shut the door, watching him uncertainly. 'Is anything broken?'

He put his foot down and stood on it experimentally. 'No, I think it's merely bruised.' He took another few steps and Annabel caught her breath finding him suddenly far too close. She backed and his eyes glinted angrily.

'Why so jumpy? What do you think I'm going to do to you?' he asked, then looked down at the deep lapels of her robe as she hastily clutched at them, pulling them together to hide the glimpse of her bare breasts he might have got.

'Are you alone here?' Sam snarled, and her eyes nervously lifted and fell again.

'Why?' she hedged. His question had made her far too deeply aware of the silence in the house, the intimacy of being here alone with him. He was taller, more powerful than she remembered; she felt confronted with some indefinable threat. What on earth is wrong with me? she thought, conscious of her hot flush and restless eyes.

'I wondered why you were so edgy,' he said with an odd, restrained hostility. 'You weren't this nervous when you were at my cottage.'

'My parents will be back any minute,' she lied, wishing he would go.

'So you are alone?' He didn't move and he was so close she almost felt she could hear the beating of his heart; she could definitely hear the irregular drag of his breathing—he sounded as if he had run here against the wind.

Why didn't he go? Why was he still standing there, staring at her as if he had never seen her before? Sunlight picked out the tautness of his cheekbones, their angular strength beneath his stretched skin giving those grey eyes an emphasised depth and darkness. She had never noticed before how black his pupils were, how fathomless and lustrous they were; she could stare down into them as if into the centre of the earth.

'You ought to dry that hair,' he said, absently, putting out a hand to touch the wet red coils hanging around her face, and she felt her throat close in shock as his fingers slid down over her hair to her throat, making a pulse beat fiercely in the vein in her neck.

'I will,' she muttered. 'When you've gone.'

He snatched his hand away as if her skin burnt it. 'Yes, of course,' he said, flushing. 'I must find Draycott—at the golf course, you said?'

'Yes, you know where it is?' Their eyes met and she grimaced. 'Yes, of course you do, I keep forgetting how well you know Blackstone.' She moved towards the door and her robe slid open at the thigh. She knew he noticed that and turned slightly to hide the glimpse of her bare skin from him, willing him to go quickly.

He leaned on the door, preventing her from

opening it, and looked down at her. 'I've given the problem of Draycott a good deal of thought,' he said coolly. 'You're right, he is too valuable to lose, but he needs to be supervised. I've decided to work with him myself for a while.'

She caught her breath. 'At the laboratories?'

'Naturally, where else?' He watched her. 'You don't seem too happy about that. You hoped I'd let you work with him, I suppose? Well, I don't think you're quite up to the job of keeping an eye on Draycott. He would still be running the experiments, and you aren't trained to recognise the danger levels in what he's dealing with—I am! I doubt if he'd listen to your advice, anyway, even if you could judge when he was taking a risk. He'll listen to me.' His tone grimly promised that and she nodded, realising he was right.

'It may take months, though,' she said hesitantly. 'What about the London end of the business? I mean, if you're going to be in Norfolk working in the laboratories, who will run the London end of things?'

'I can delegate all that, that's no problem,' he said flatly.

Annabel made a puzzled face, remembering that he had told her that he much preferred working in the laboratories to working in London, but that he had no choice. What had changed?

'Are you coming back to Blackstone for good, then?' she asked. 'Will you be starting a new project?'

His mouth was tense and crooked, his eyes hard. 'I doubt it. Oh, I used to work at full stretch, full of ideas—scientists are like writers in one way, they're creative, they constantly extend what they know and get flashes of intuition about something else, something they have no evidence for but which a hunch tells them exists, and then they have to work their way towards proving their hunch is right. Usually, proving a new idea is one-tenth hunch to nine-tenths slog. But sometimes that creativity dries up; there are no flashes of intuition, no hunches. You get a blockage somewhere in your head and there's nothing you can do about it but wait and hope that one day it will clear.'

'Is that why you've been working up in London for the last few years? Waiting for a blockage in your mind to clear?' Annabel asked with sudden sympathy. She hadn't suspected that Sam Jerrard might have problems of this kind, he seemed so sure of himself.

He nodded, a little nerve jumping in his lean cheek. She sensed that he half-wished he hadn't confided in her. A man like Sam Jerrard must hate to admit to a weakness.

'Will I be able to get a cup of coffee and a sandwich at this golf club?' he asked, changing the subject abruptly, looking at his watch. 'I've driven down from town without lunch and I'm beginning to feel hungry.'

'I think they do a lunch there, but I'm not sure about sandwiches in the afternoon,' Annabel answered slowly, frowning. 'I could make you some tea—there's some sliced ham in the fridge and some salad. Would you like to wait for Charlie here? He and my brother will come back for tea, I expect, and, anyway, you might miss them on the road from the golf club. They only play for an hour or so.'

He hesitated. 'Sure I wouldn't be a nuisance?' His eyes held a mocking gleam and he smiled. 'You won't be scared, being alone with me?'

She turned and walked into the kitchen to hide her quick flush. 'Tea or coffee?' she asked over her shoulder as he followed her.

'Whichever is convenient.'

'Either suits me—which would you prefer?'

'Tea, then,' he said and watched her filling the kettle and plugging it into the electric socket.

'You won't tell Draycott what I told you, will you?' he asked curtly.

Annabel turned, smiling gently. 'Of course I won't.' She sliced some bread with deft expertise, got out ham and a bowl of salad and made some sandwiches, aware that he was staring, apparently fascinated by every movement. What was he thinking about? She knew he was not thinking about her; his eyes were too fixed.

'I envy Draycott,' he said suddenly, as she placed the plate of sandwiches on the kitchen table. Annabel stared at him, baffled, and his mouth twisted. 'Maybe that's why I've been so tough on him. He needed a short, sharp lesson; he's far too reckless, but I resent him a little, too. He's good, damned good, and I suppose I'm jealous because I've lost it for the moment. I know just how he must feel—the excitement, the constant ferment of ideas, the pressure to get it all down on paper, to know if you're right or wrong. Yes, I can't help envying the man.'

'You've done some brilliant work, though!' protested Annabel.

He looked grim. 'In the past,' he said shortly. 'I
ran out of steam and I don't know if I'll ever get
going again—if I thought it was just a matter of
waiting, for a year or two, I'd wait patiently, but I
hate the idea of being nothing but an administrator
for the rest of my working life. I'll suffocate up in
London.'

Annabel considered him, her brow furrowed.
'That's why you transferred to London? Because
you'd run out of ideas?'

'I was in between projects and someone had to
set up the London end; I felt I couldn't trust
anyone else at the time. Now, I've got a good team
working with me up there, I can hand over to my
second-in-command without a qualm—but it's
four years since I did any original research and I
don't know if I'm ever going to do any again.'

He sat down as she poured him a cup of tea.
'Thank you, this is very good of you,' he said. 'I'm
really hungry, I'd forgotten to eat, stupid of me.'

'Will you excuse me while I dry my hair and get
dressed?'

'Yes, of course,' he said, and Annabel left him
to eat his meal in peace. She took a quarter of an
hour to get ready and by the time she had rejoined
Sam Jerrard he had finished his sandwiches and
was standing by the kitchen window looking into
the garden watching a robin. He looked round as
she came into the room, the hard lines of his face
smoothed out into a sort of peace.

'That was quick,' he complimented, running an
assessing gaze over her glowing hair and the white-
collared, navy blue pleated dress she wore. It had a
demure neatness which had made Patrick call it

her schoolgirl outfit, but the contrast with her vivid flame hair and green eyes usually made men look more than twice, and Sam Jerrard didn't hurry in his observation of her. 'You look dangerously sedate,' he murmured drily.

'Contradiction in terms?' Annabel retorted.

'You are all contradictions,' Sam informed her.

She suddenly remembered Denise Keiron and the laughter faded out of her face. 'How's your fiancée?' she asked coldly and Sam looked blank, as if he had forgotten Denise, too.

His dark lashes flickered, he looked away, frowning. 'I haven't seen Denise for some time—not since I left for Brussels. I must ring her, I suppose.' He sounded far from eager, but Annabel was relieved to hear a key in the front door and then Patrick and Charlie stamping back into the house, noisy with good temper and exercise. They had come just at the right moment.

'I'll leave you to talk to Charlie,' she said. 'You can talk to him in our sitting room, if you like.'

Sam moved towards the door and Annabel sat down at the table, her mind absorbed. She had forgotten he was engaged to another woman for a while; stupid of her. She wouldn't forget again.

CHAPTER SEVEN

ANNABEL saw Charlie in the canteen at the laboratories next day. He was eating the cheap dish of the day, a spicy prawn curry with rice and sliced bananas, and staring at it vacantly, obviously miles away. He jumped when she joined him at the table, his hunted expression making her laugh.

'It's only me! Who did you think it was?'

Charlie lowered his voice to a confidential whisper. 'He's here. He's going over my notes and he keeps asking me questions. I came to lunch to get away from him. I don't know if I'm going to be able to stand working with him for months on end. The man's terrifying.'

'It's your project,' soothed Annabel. 'If he didn't believe in you, he wouldn't be prepared to work with you—it's a great compliment, Charlie.' She had chosen a cottage cheese and pineapple salad from the counter. Charlie watched her begin to eat it, his expression unconvinced.

'That's all very well, you don't have to face him. It's like having your teeth pulled without an anaesthetic. I still can't believe it's happening to me. I didn't think he'd insist on keeping an eye on me himself—it makes me feel I'm back at school. I'm even beginning to wonder if my research isn't all a pipe-dream.'

'Don't be silly. He wouldn't be here if it was just

that,' Annabel looked around the canteen and saw Alison Morris at another table, drinking her coffee. Annabel waved to her on impulse and Alison came over, carrying her cup carefully.

'Have you seen the big boss yet, Alison?' asked Annabel cheerfully and the other girl sat down, shaking her head, with her eyes on Charlie's disconsolate expression.

'No, but I think it's mean of him to walk in and take over Charlie's research,' she said passionately and Charlie looked up at once. 'You've done all the basic work, now he's snatching the glory,' Alison added, her brown eyes soothing to Charlie's wounded feelings. She was a pretty girl, yet it was not a memorable face. Her pink and white skin and curly hair gave her a faintly doll-like look.

'He is rather high-handed,' Charlie shrugged, trying to be casual.

'I'll say!' Alison agreed. 'And I thought he was so gorgeously sexy! He really took me in; I don't like him at all now.'

'I thought he made you feel dizzy?' teasd Annabel deliberately and Alison turned bright pink.

'That was before I knew what a snake he was!' She gazed at Charlie with a sympathy he obviously found delightful. 'I think it's a shame!'

Annabel carefully changed the subject. 'Have you seen that film at the Odeon? Patrick told me it was very good; he saw it on Wednesday. I meant to go but I've been too busy.'

'I meant to go, too,' agreed Alison. 'Oh, I forgot—did you enjoy the wedding on Saturday? Did everything go well?'

'Apart from the best man forgetting he was supposed to have the ring, it went off very well,' Annabel said, smiling. She finished her salad while Charlie and Alison talked about the wedding reception, then looked at her watch, getting up. 'Oh, I forgot—I have to check something dead on two o'clock. I must fly.'

Rather reluctantly, Alison half-rose to go with her, but Annabel threw her a smile and said, 'Finish your coffee, Alison!' She hurried out of the canteen, leaving the other two alone at the table, and made her way back to the lab. She hadn't been lying; she had to run a whole series of checks on one of the growth experiments, but she was also keen to leave Charlie and Alison alone together. She was conducting some private research of her own.

Charlie might not have noticed Alison much before today, but Annabel intended to throw them together as often as possible from now onwards. She suspected that, with Alison's encouragement, Charlie would get around to asking the other girl out sooner or later. He was used to having his life arranged for him by his mother and was inclined to drift into relationships from sheer propinquity, but he was also susceptible to any form of sympathy, and Alison's warm support just now had made his eyes brighten. Annabel had been vaguely aware that the other girl liked Charlie. He was a very good-looking, rugged guy with an athletic figure. Those buttery curls and blue eyes, the broad shoulders and long, slim legs had always attracted female admirers, but the way Charlie hung around Annabel had daunted other girls as much as it kept men at arm's length from Annabel.

If Annabel was to wean him away from herself, she had to distract him with someone else, and Alison seemed a nice girl with a soft heart. She would be just right for Charlie.

While she was examining slides under a microscope to evaluate the growth on them, Annabel wryly wondered if Sam Jerrard was aware of Charlie's resentment at losing control of his personal project. Charlie had already forgotten why Sam had come down from London to take charge of the experiment; he had buried the memory of the explosion and his own dismissal. It was typical of Charlie; he had all the obstinacy of the weak and the convenient memory of the spoilt. Sam Jerrard might begin to wish he had never agreed to let Charlie stay on.

She was alone in the lab an hour later, carefully entering the results of the checks into one of the computers, when she heard the soft swish of the door and glanced over her shoulder to see Sam Jerrard behind her. He was wearing a white coat, like her own, and looked subtly different to the way he had always looked before when she saw him in dark suits or a sweater and cord trousers.

'Draycott here?' he asked curtly.

She shook her head. He could see that Charlie wasn't in the room; he didn't need to ask. She was tempted to retort, 'Do you think I've got him hidden in a cupboard?' but something in that dark profile made her hold her tongue.

Sam thrust his hands down into the pockets of the white coat, his mouth compressed.

'Something wrong?' Annabel asked cagily. He looked furious.

'Draycott keeps vanishing,' Sam erupted. 'Every time I look round, he's missing. What does he think he's playing at? I need to check through those notes with him and his isn't the easiest handriting in the world to decipher. I'm not surprised he keeps getting the wrong result. He puts decimal points in without rhyme or reason and his scribble verges on shorthand at times.'

Annabel turned round on the rotating stool, running a hand over her hair and grimacing. 'Try to understand,' she said quite quietly. 'Charlie is finding it tough to have you taking over from him. Just give him time to get used to the idea. You'll find him quite amenable in a few days.'

'Do you?' he asked with barbed mockery and she did a double take.

'What?'

'Find him easy to manage? You've got him eating out of your hand, I suppose? Don't you find that sort of relationship a bit tame, or are you the sort of female who likes to rule the roost?' His cool stare lifted to her hair, which was turned to a blazing crown by the sunlight through the laboratory window. 'It must be that red hair,' he decided.

Annabel had been feeling sympathetic towards him ever since she saw Charlie in the canteen and realised that Sam Jerrard was getting a rough ride in the process of taking over Charlie's project. His admission to her that he hadn't been able to come up with any original research of his own for some years had softened her view of him, but now she felt her earlier hostility towards him churning around inside her again. It wasn't easy to feel sympathetic to the man. He made her nerves bristle.

'If you try the other labs you may find Charlie in one of them,' she said coldly, turning back to her computer.

He didn't go. He came closer and leant over to stare at the screen on which her string of results was printed. Annabel stiffened, aware that his lean cheek almost touched her own.

'What's this? The grass research?'

She nodded without answering, her body going rigid as she felt his arm going round her to let his hand rest on the solid plastic shelf on which the computers rested. Out of the corner of an eye she watched him rapidly skim a glance down the figures on the screen. Sunlight showed her the grainy texture of his skin, the hardness of the cheekbones underneath it, the warm, male curve of his mouth and the strong jawline under that. It was not a face one could dismiss or forget; it was memorable and disturbing and Annabel's pulse-rate picked up alarmingly.

'Interesting results,' he murmured.

'I think we're on the right track,' Annabel agreed huskily, hoping he couldn't hear her increased heartbeat. It was stupid to be this aware of any man.

'There's a lot of interest from the Arabs on this one,' Sam said, half turning to look at her. 'In the desert, grass blows away before it has had a chance to root itself firmly—if we can only solve the problem of finding a grass that can live in sand without blowing away with every strong wind we'll be making a real contribution.' He smiled wryly. 'Not to mention a profit!'

'We've still got a good deal of experiment to do on it,' she said, trying to sound calm, and wondering if she was crazy to feel that although on the surface all they were talking about was a scientific experiment there was quite a different dialogue going on at another level. Her eyes wouldn't be dragged away from their fascinated study of him and her skin and blood reacted to his presence as if he was some strange substance to which they were intensely sensitive.

'Oh, of course,' he said absently, staring back, his pupils gleaming molten black in the sunlight, a liquid jet which made the grey of the iris seem to darken.

She watched his mouth move, barely hearing what he said. 'You enjoy the work?' she deciphered, a moment after he had spoken, and somehow managed to nod.

'Very much; I'd hate to work anywhere else now.' Her voice sounded unfamiliar: unsteady and dry. She moistened her lips nervously and Sam Jerrard's stare dropped to watch, making her withdraw the pink tip of her tongue with a faint gasp of shock.

One of the lab technicians came through the door and Sam straightened, his face changing. 'I'll look for Draycott elsewhere, then,' he said and the other man quickly told him that Charlie was in the research garden.

'I just saw him go into the greenhouse,' the technician said and Sam thanked him and strode out.

At half-past four, Annabel went down to the canteen to have a cup of tea and saw Gwen Bridge at one of the other tables, eating a sandwich as if it was made of sawdust, her thin, sallow face set in irritable lines. Annabel joined her and was given a sour stare.

'Oh, it's you!'

'Yes,' Annabel agreed, determined not to be put off by Gwen's unwelcoming manner. 'I want to talk to you.'

'I'm in no mood to listen to more special pleading on behalf of your young man; he's caused me enough trouble already!' Gwen finished her sandwich and pushed away the plate, scowling.

'That isn't what I want to talk about—I want to now why you followed me and Mr Jerrard down to that cottage and took the rotor arm from his car,' Annabel said belligerently and saw the other woman's eyes flicker.

'Who says I did?'

'It has to be you—it wasn't me and I don't think it was Mr Jerrard, so that only leaves one candidate.'

'I don't know what you're talking about,' Gwen said, belatedly.

'Oh, yes, you do! I know you did it, I just want to know why!'

'You're crazy,' Gwen said, getting up.

Annabel caught her arm. 'Do you want me to tell Mr Jerrard who helped me stow away in his car and who tipped off Denise Keiron about the cottage?'

Gwen's mouth thinned and she looked at Annabel with intense dislike. 'You little bitch! He wouldn't believe you. I'd tell him it was all lies.'

'Oh, I think he'd believe me, especially if Denise Keiron admitted it was you who gave her that address!' Annabel mentally hoped she was right about that; she was gambling that Gwen had been responsible for Denise and her father turning up at the cottage at precisely the right moment, and she would look very silly if she was wrong.

Gwen hesitated, staring down at her, then abruptly sat down again and leaned across the table to mutter. 'You haven't got any proof of any of that! And you gave me your word you'd never tell him I helped you. What difference does it make to you, anyway? Your boyfriend got his job back, didn't he? What more do you want?'

'I'm just curious,' Annabel said, lying. It was more than that—she needed to know for sure that it was Gwen who had taken that rotor arm and stranded her and Sam at the cottage.

Gwen shrugged her thin shoulders, drawing her lower lip inwards between her teeth. 'Okay, I took the rotor arm, and I had followed you and Sam—I already knew the address, I found out years ago, although I never let on to him that I knew it. He was determined that it should be a secret; I knew he'd be furious if he knew I'd found out. Sam's funny about privacy, but I hadn't any intention of telling anyone else; I just liked to know where he was.' Her eyes had a darkness in them which made Annabel freeze with abrupt understanding and sympathy.

'You sabotaged the car so that I'd still be there when Denise Keiron arrived, I suppose?' she said quite gently and saw a wave of dark red colour wash up Gwen's face.

'What if I did? She isn't right for him, she won't make him happy, she's a spoilt little bitch and as selfish as hell. Sam would be miserable with her. All she cares about is money and herself; she doesn't give a damn for him.'

'But if he loves her . . .' Annabel began, appalled by the suffering she could glimpse in the other woman's face. Gwen shook violently.

'Love her?' she spat out. 'Of course he doesn't love her! She's not his type. There's nothing in that head of hers but clothes and spending money. Sam's a genius, with a brilliant mind; how could he possibly be happy with a girl like her?'

Annabel looked down, she couldn't bear to see the expression in Gwen's eyes. Every word the other woman said gave her away, betrayed her feelings for Sam Jerrard. Did he know how she felt? Annabel suddenly remembered that Charlie had said something about Gwen being possessive about her boss. If it had percolated through to Charlie, surely Sam Jerrard must have guessed?

'But he did ask her to marry him,' Annabel murmured. 'Why else should he . . .?'

'She's rich, isn't she?' Gwen retorted bitterly. 'And her father pressured Sam into proposing—I heard him, myself, dropping hints as big as houses about how much money the girl would have when she married and what he'd do for his son-in-law. Sam couldn't very well miss what was on old Keiron's mind.'

'And Mr Jerrard was ready to let himself be bought?' Annabel was sickened, her mouth wry with distaste. She hadn't thought it of Sam Jerrard. It had baffled her what a man like him could see in a blonde barracuda like Denise Keiron but she certainly hadn't suspected that he was marrying the girl for her money. 'What on earth made you try to interfere? You should have let him sell himself, if that was what he wanted to do,' she said angrily.

'I couldn't,' Gwen muttered. 'Someone had to rescue Sam.'

'He didn't want to be rescued! And it didn't work, anyway—he made me hide. She never knew I was there.'

Gwen's eyes narrowed. 'She didn't see you?'

'No. Mr Jerrard saw her Rolls Royce coming along the road and he made me hide upstairs until she'd gone.'

Gwen breathed, staring at nothing in silence, then said, 'I wondered how he'd managed to talk her round. I haven't seen him for the last couple of weeks, of course, he's been in Brussels, and as soon as he got back he handed over to his deputy and came down here.' Her hands clenched and she put them down on her lap out of sight. 'I'm working for someone else now. Sam says he doesn't need a secretary for the moment, so he's transferred me to the new boss, in London. I only came down to bring him some letters and papers to sign. I won't be seeing him for quite a while, I suppose.' Each word was charged with pain and Annabel was very uncomfortable, listening to her.

What could she say? She could hardly say, 'I'm sorry,' although she was, very sorry for the other woman. Gwen would hate to realise how much she had betrayed.

The other woman got up awkwardly, collecting

her bag and a pair of brown kid gloves. 'I must go,' she said, then gave Annabel a cold glance. 'You won't tell Sam anything?' It was a peculiar mixture of demand and pleading, and Annabel hadn't the heart to deny it.

She shook her head and Gwen walked away, her heels tapping on the tiled floor. Annabel watched her until she was out of sight, thinking grimly that she wished she hadn't seen her at all, wished she hadn't tackled her about the stolen rotor arm. She should have ignored Gwen, let sleeping dogs lie. She wouldn't now have a very distasteful picture of Sam Jerrard. Was it true, though? Had he proposed to the Keiron girl just because her father was rich? It didn't add up with everything else she knew about the man; Sam Jerrard did not look like a fortune hunter or a cold-blooded opportunist. He was maddening, he was tough and domineering, but she hadn't suspected that he might be marrying Denise Keiron for her money, and after all that Gwen had told her she felt she didn't want to see Sam again for a long time.

He was very busy working in the laboratories with Charlie all that week and Annabel managed somehow to stay out of his path. She had a fixed daily routine which couldn't be altered except by prior arrangement with another member of the staff who took over her various jobs. It was a tranquil existence and Annabel was relieved that Sam Jerrard didn't break in upon it again. Charlie seemed to have accepted the inevitable; she didn't have to listen much to him either. Or was he taking his grievances to Alison Morris now? she wondered with amusement.

On Friday of that week, Annabel had to have a lift to work from her brother because her own car was being serviced by the local garage. Patrick couldn't pick her up in the evening, but Charlie had promised to give her a lift home. Towards five o'clock it began to rain and Annabel watched the darkening skies wondering whether to risk running into Sam Jerrard by going into the lab where he and Charlie were working, to remind Charlie that he was taking her home, or whether to wait for Charlie at the entrance and hope he hadn't forgotten. He was more than capable of it; he had a mind like a sieve.

Annabel hadn't brought a raincoat or an umbrella, and her mustardy-yellow wool suit would be ruined if it got soaked in the cascading rain she saw through the windows, so when Charlie hadn't appeared by a quarter to six she reluctantly went across the corridor to peer into the other lab. She saw Sam Jerrard's dark head bent over a microscope, a green-shaded lamp casting a shifting pattern of light across the white coat he wore. There was no sign of Charlie, or anyone else. On Friday evenings, everyone left early if they could.

Annabel began to pull the door softly shut but Sam Jerrard must have picked up some tiny sound because he suddenly swung round to stare at her.

'Sorry, I didn't mean to disturb you,' stammered Annabel, wishing his hearing wasn't so acute. 'I was looking for Charlie.'

'He left ten minutes ago.'

She involuntarily grimaced. Charlie had forgotten he was picking her up! Sam watched, his black brows lifting.

'What's the matter?'

'Nothing, it's just . . . I may find him in the car park,' she said, walking out and beginning to run down the corridor as soon as she was out of Sam Jerrard's sight. When she reached the glass swing doors leading out into the car park she saw at once that Charlie's car had gone. In fact, all the cars had gone except one which she recognised grimly as Sam Jerrard's. Annabel turned back face set, and went to look for a phone—she would have to ring Patrick and ask him to come and fetch her.

Sam Jerrard met her in the corridor. He was wearing a pale Burberry trench-coat, the lapels standing up around his face and the belt hanging loose. 'Has Draycott gone?' he asked, glancing past her into the rain-swept car park whose black tarmac glistened under the street lamps, and Annabel nodded without speaking.

'No car?' He was quick-witted, she had to admit that. It was obvious there was no other car in sight but his.

'My brother will come and get me,' she said. 'The caretaker doesn't lock up until six and Patrick will be here by then.'

'I'll take you home,' Sam said.

'It's okay, no need for you to go out of your way. Patrick won't mind picking me up on his way home.'

'Why do you argue so much?' Sam demanded with an impatient stare. 'You waste a lot of time.' He looked her up and down. 'Are you ready to leave now?' He apparently read the answer in her face because his hand shot out and gripped her arm, guiding her back towards the swing doors. 'Wait here and I'll bring my car over to you, then you won't get so wet,' he said, and darted out into the rain. She stood in the foyer, watching him running across the tarmac, his hair immediately saturated and plastered to his head. His trench-coat darkened with spots of rain long before he unlocked his car and slid behind the wheel. His lights flashed on, cutting through the shadows, and a moment later he pulled up in front of the building and Annabel ran out and climbed in beside him.

Sam watched her pull the seat belt over her body, then he took the metal clip and slotted it firmly into place. Annabel snatched her own hand away the second she felt his fingers brush her own. Sam made no comment, but he looked at her through his lashes, observing the colour in her cheeks with derisive eyes.

He drove out of the car park and turned left, feeding his car deftly into the slow-moving traffic.

'Are you living at your cottage while you're working here?' she asked nervously a moment later, but he shook his head.

'It was too far to drive every morning. No, I've rented a flat in Holme Park.'

Surprised, she said, 'That's quite near us!'

'I know,' he said drily, with a flick of his long lashes. 'I'm Norfolk born, remember—I know Blackstone like the back of my hand.' He drove in silence for a moment, staring through the flickering windscreen wipers at the wet, black road. 'It's nice to be back,' he said abruptly.

'Your family had a farm here, didn't they?'

'Still do,' he said. 'My father died last year, but my younger brother still farms the land—it's a mixed farm, part arable, part sheep. He makes a living but it's hard work.'

'You didn't want to farm?'

He smiled crookedly, staring ahead. 'I always wanted to be a scientist. I was one of the lucky ones who know what they want and can get it.'

Annabel sighed. 'Yes.' He was very much a man who went for what he wanted; he didn't need to tell her that. It was written all over him, in every line of that lean, tough body and in the cool, assured grey eyes.

Sam glanced at her quickly. 'What about you? Are you doing what you wanted to do?'

She hesitated. 'I was always fascinated by science.'

'But you didn't want to become a scientist? You didn't go to university to study it, did you? Didn't you want to or . . .'

'We couldn't afford it,' Annabel said shortly.

He frowned. 'All those brothers?'

Yes, he was quick-witted and shrewd, he read between the lines and heard what you did not say. She didn't answer and he took one hand off the wheel and touched her lightly.

'I'm sorry.'

Startled, she looked out of the side window, freezing, and he took his hand away. After a pause Annabel muttered, 'It was my decision—they'd have found the money somehow, if I'd asked them to, but I was the youngest and they'd done so much already, I couldn't let them scrimp and save for another three years, just for me.'

'You're a very close family?' guessed Sam and she laughed, relaxing a little as they turned into her road and she knew that any minute now her ordeal would be over. Driving alone with Sam Jerrard in this car had been a fraught experience; he had a worrying effect on Annabel's pulse-rate even when he was being kind.

'We're very close. I have wonderful parents.'

He pulled up outside her gate and stared at the house curiously. 'I must meet them sometime.'

Annabel flinched involuntarily, horrified by the idea of her family seeing her with him. They knew her too well; they might guess that she was far from indifferent to Sam Jerrard and she couldn't bear them to probe or watch her or smile.

Sam shot her a hard stare. 'But you'd rather I didn't?'

How did he read her mind like this? she wondered grimly, trying to turn her face into a mask he couldn't penetrate, even with those x-ray eyes of his.

'I didn't say . . .' she began, flushing.

'You didn't have to!' he interrupted tersely, his mouth suddenly a hard, cold line. 'You're not hard to interpret; your face is a give-away.'

She stiffened, unbelting herself. 'Thanks for the lift, Mr Jerrard, it was very kind of you to go to so much trouble.'

'Do your family like Draycott?' He caught her arm as she began to get out of the car, holding her back.

'My brother Patrick is Charlie's best friend, always has been,' she said, poised to flee the instant he let go of her, her body turned away from him.

'And they want you to marry him?' he guessed again and she angrily shook her head.

'They've never even raised the subject!'

'But they keep pushing you in his direction,' Sam drawled, his face sardonic, and she resented the derision in his smile.

'They don't do anything of the kind! Charlie's a family friend, that's all.'

'He's just a friend, a good friend,' he jeered. 'Now why don't I believe you?'

Furiously, Annabel snapped, 'How should I know? I don't give a damn whether you believe me or not. What makes my private life your business, anyway? I don't keep making comments on your fiancée; I mind my own business, even though I . . .' She pulled herself up, biting her lip before she had let loose the barbed remarks she had been about to make on Denise Keiron.

Sam pulled her right round to face, him, his grey eyes narrowed and glinting. 'Even though you . . . what?'

She looked down mutinously, brushing a shaky hand over her faintly damp red hair. 'Nothing. Let go. I must go in or my family will think . . .'

'What will they think?' he asked softly, mockingly. 'That I'm making love to you?'

She fought to halt the hot rush of colour in her face. 'They won't think anything of the sort!'

'Do you sit out in Draycott's car when he brings you home?'

The dry question made her look up, eyes wide, face startled. Sam was far too close, bending over

her, his hands pinning her shoulders to the seat
his eyes fixed on the tremulous line of her mouth.

'What on earth do you see in him?' he muttered

Annabel lost her head, confused by his nearnes.
and her own tumultuous reaction to him. 'Don'
. . .' she whispered, pushing him away, and heard
Sam's angry intake of breath.

'Don't what?' he snarled. 'Don't do this?' He
kissed her before she could turn her head away, hi.
mouth forcibly taking her lips with an insistence
that paralysed her.

Her eyes shut, she couldn't breathe, she couldn'
even think. The kiss devoured, suffocated, wrung
out of her a response she was unable to control or
conceal. Her body slackened, arching under him in
a yielding curve as her arms went round his neck
and then Sam's mouth softened and moved with
seductive slowness. She felt his fingers moving
through her hair, stroking her nape, caressing her
stretched throat, the feel of them so sensitive, sc
sensuous, that she trembled violently.

Her ears drummed with the sound of her own
blood; her hand moved up his taut face, her
fingertips tracing the bone structure under that
flushed skin, crawling down over his lowered lids.
brushing his lashes. Her skin seemed to cling to
his, the whorled pads at the end of her fingers
imprinting themselves on him and absorbing his
living texture into her blood stream.

Sam pushed his mouth down into her neck,
breathing raggedly, his hands touching her.
moving under the short jacket of her woollen suit
and exploring the soft flesh.

Annabel had never felt anything like this fierce,

stabbing desire—she knew now that she wanted him, that her body needed this contact with his, even through her own emotions scared her senseless.

Sam lifted his head and looked at her through half-closed eyes, his lips parted. She was feverish, distraught, shuddering as the silence stretched between them—a silence which said more than words could do, admitting the intensity of what their bodies had felt.

Annabel couldn't bear it. She pushed him away, almost in tears, and before he knew what she meant to do she was out of the car and running up the path, trembling from head to foot.

CHAPTER EIGHT

ANNABEL blundered into the house and straight into her father, who steadied her, laughing, then looked down, his face changing to an expression of concern.

'What's the matter, Annie?' He looked through the open door to where Sam was just driving off. 'Who was that? What did he do to you?' Mr Walsh was immediately anxious, frowning, his imagination leaping to heaven knew what conclusions, and a dangerous glare coming into his eyes.

Annabel had often thought how lucky she was to be part of a large and loving family, but tonight she wished she lived alone, away from such all-seeing eyes.

'Oh, I just had a row with someone,' she muttered, trying to escape upstairs to her own room where she could howl to her heart's content.

'Who? A row? Over what?'

'It doesn't matter, Dad!'

'It does, you know,' her father said, producing a large clean hankie and drying her face with it the way he had when she was a very small girl. 'Blow,' he said, putting it to her nose.

'Oh, Dad!' Annabel said, ready to cry again.

'Did he hurt you?' Mr Walsh asked gently and instead of crying she laughed wildly.

'Depends what you mean ... he didn't try to ravish me, if that's what you're hinting at!'

Her father looked both shocked and relieved at the same time, making little protesting noises. 'Of course not, I didn't think anything of the sort—but who is he? I didn't recognise that car, is this someone new?' Then, as she might have expected, in a reproachful voice, 'What about Charlie? Where does he fit in? Does he know about this other man?'

Annabel helplessly gazed at him, shaking her head and torn between hysterical laugher and angry weeping. 'You're making my head go round, Dad! Stop asking questions, for heaven's sake!'

'It isn't like you to be secretive about your young men,' Mr Walsh murmured curiously. 'When are we going to meet him?'

Annabel gave up. 'He isn't my young man and you aren't going to meet him!' She turned and darted away up the stairs before he could launch another flotilla of questions at her, and felt him staring after her in perturbed silence. As she ran across the landing she heard Patrick whistling in the bathroom and even through a solid oak door she could smell his new after-shave being splashed on heavily. Patrick was making himself desirable for his latest conquest—there had been quite a few over the past few years, though none of them seemed to have mattered. But her parents didn't constantly quiz Patrick; they weren't worried about whatever he might get up to while he was on a date, nor did they wait up for him to make sure he wasn't too late. Either they were afraid that Annabel would turn into a pumpkin after midnight, or that the witching hour would weaken her defences against marauding men, but whenever she got home late she found either her parents or one of her brothers waiting up for her. Protective affection could go too far, she felt, bolting herself into her bedroom in case one of them tried to follow her.

She sank down on her bed, wrapping her arms around herself. She felt peculiarly cold suddenly, although she had been feverish with heat while she was in Sam's arms in the car. The dressing-table mirror opposite showed her a pale, drawn face and tumbled, ruffled red hair. Her green eyes glittered, but the skin beneath them was shadowed and her mouth was quivering.

She sat in silence, facing one fact which she should have faced long ago. She had fallen in love with a man who was engaged to someone else.

She closed her eyes to shut out that disturbing reflection; it gave away too much. I can't be in love with him, she thought. I don't even like him. Her mind surged with memories of Sam laughing, Sam talking about his work, his family, the birds he loved to draw and watch. Annabel bit her lower lip. Why lie to herself? She liked Sam—oh, yes, he was maddening at times, infuriatingly arrogant and domineering, totally without scruples of any kind, of course, or he would never have kissed her in the first place. He had no right to go around kissing people. He was going to marry Denise Keiron; she had exclusive rights over his kisses and Sam must know it, which made him a man Annabel knew she ought to despise, yet she couldn't help liking him. That didn't mean she had to go even further and love him, of course, and she clenched her fists and pushed them into her eyes as if to grind all thought of him out of her head.

'I am not in love,' she said aloud then froze, listening to the lying echo. The house seemed horribly quiet. Anyone could have heard her.

'I'm talking to myself, she thought; that's the first sign of madness, isn't it? What was love but madness? Especially when someone fell in love with a forbidden man who belonged to another woman, even if the woman in question was someone you disliked intensely, and who certainly wasn't good enough to marry Sam Jerrard.

She heard Patrick going downstairs a few minutes later and unbolted her door to rush into the empty bathroom, which she occupied for the next half hour, taking a long, relaxing bubble bath. By the time she went downstairs she felt more normal, but as soon as she went into the kitchen a silence fell and everyone turned to stare at her, making it glaringly apparent that they had been talking about her. Annabel felt herself blush and was furious.

'What's for supper, Mum?' she asked aggressively, daring them to say anything.

'Ham and eggs,' Mrs Walsh said and Patrick straightened his tie and told them he was having dinner out with his girlfriend.

'You going out, Annie?' he asked casually.

Into a charged silence Annabel said that she was staying in that evening. Her parents looked relieved but Patrick teased her. 'On a Friday night? Charlie said something about seeing the film at the Odeon.'

'Not with me,' Annabel said tersely, walking out

of the room to go and watch some television, but if she thought that that would deter Patrick's probing she was wrong because he followed her and perched on the arm of her chair in brotherly concern, tousling her damp hair.

'Had a row with Charlie?'

'No.' Annabel kept her eyes on the current affairs programme she was pretending to watch.

'Come on, you can tell me—who was the guy?'

'Nobody,' Annabel said.

'Is he that special?'

'Go away, Patrick,' she wailed, pushing him off the chair. He gave her a dignified look and left at last, recognising defeat.

Annabel spent the weekend trying, not very successfully, to convince herself that she was not in love with Sam Jerrard, and, with rather more success, to convince her parents that she was just a little ray of sunshine without a care in the world. Wearing a bright smile all day was exhausting. She would have been glad to get back to work on Monday if she hadn't been dreading seeing Sam again.

She spent the first hour in the laboratory talking to the more junior members of the staff, who needed frequent supervision; checking over the trays of slides on which they would be working and showing one of them how to enter a complex string of results. Once they were all busy, she walked through the side door into the experimental garden. The wind was quite cold today; it was pleasant to get out of it and into the sunlit greenhouse where she began inspecting the growth of a row of seedlings set out in carefully labelled trays.

On a Monday morning the laundry delivered clean white coats for each member of staff. Today, Annabel's coat had been over-starched to such an extent that she had had to force the buttons through their holes, and every time she stretched forward she crackled quite alarmingly.

She began noting down the rates of growth in each tray; entering them in neat columns in a big black ledger. It was dangerously easy to make a mistake if you tried to hurry; she had learnt a long time ago that you had to work slowly and carefully on these precise and often tedious tasks. Absolute accuracy was essential. The scientists working on these projects relied on the information garnered from this data: one decimal point in the wrong place and the consequences could be disastrous.

One wall of the greenhouse was made of strange, green glass meant to exclude some rays of the sun and alter the conditions under which the seedlings grew. Annabel was collecting some cuttings for study in the laboratory when through that wall she saw a tall figure in a white coat swim into view, like a denizen of the deep ocean, his black hair given a blue gleam like a starling's wing, his skin greenish and his eyes startlingly brilliant. She froze as he walked towards the greenhouse door, opened it and looked through a climbing vine at her.

'There you are! I want to talk to you!' His tone had a cutting insistence that set her teeth on edge.

'I'm busy at the moment. Can't it wait?'

'No, it can't!' He came in, slamming the door behind him, and all the glass walls shook.

'You'll bring the place down around our ears if you do that too often!' Annabel said, a little alarmed.

'At this precise moment, nothing would give me greater pleasure!'

Her eyes widened. 'Oh! Well . . . what do you want?'

Sam leaned on one of the slatted shelves, his lithe body pretending to a negligence she did not see in his eyes. 'We both know the answer to that, don't we?' he drawled, irony in his smile, and she flushed and turned away, fumbling with the black ledger into which she had just written rows of careful figures.

'Put that down and listen to me,' Sam commanded, snatching the ledger away. 'Why did you bolt like that on Friday? I rang your home a couple of times and they kept saying you were out . . .' He broke off, watching her averted face. 'Are you listening?'

'*You* pay me,' she muttered, head bent and hands behind her like a schoolgirl. 'I'm listening, but you're wasting your time.'

'You aren't in love with Draycott!' he told her in a calmer voice a moment later.

'Aren't I?' She wasn't going to argue with him any more; she was going to use a passive force against him, digging her heels in like a recalcitrant mule.

'You wouldn't have kissed me like that if you were.' Sam chucked the ledger down and almost knocked over one of the trays of carefully nurtured seedlings. He straightened the tray, his long fingers deft, and she watched through her lashes, riveted by the graceful movement of his hands, remembering the caressing way they had touched her in his car on Friday evening.

He turned back to her, and her eyes became wary, lowering again. 'If we've settled that, can I get back to work?' she asked in dulcet tones.

Sam swore and she was startled into staring. 'Annabel,' he said huskily, then, meeting her green eyes with a demanding stare, and coming closer: 'Have dinner with me tonight. We can't talk here, someone may interrupt us any minute—we've got to be alone. Why don't we have dinner in my flat? I'll cook a special meal and then we'll talk.'

Annabel was stiff with affront and bitter with suspicion. Did he think she was totally naïve? Did he really suppose that she couldn't work out what he actually meant? He was inviting her to his flat that night for something more than dinner.

'Talk?' she queried in a voice that tinkled like icicles in the wind, then laughed angrily. 'You've got the wrong impression if you think I'm going to fall for that corny old trick. No, Mr Jerrard, I won't come to your flat tonight.' She spun on her heel and walked out of the greenhouse.

She knew he was following her, but she didn't look around, hurrying back into the main building as if the hounds of hell were on her heels. Sam caught up with her in the corridor outside her lab but just at that moment Charlie came out of the door and stopped, his face clearing. 'Oh, there you are, Annabel—I've been looking for you,' he said without noticing Sam at first. 'I've got to see you,' Charlie went on, then stopped mid-sentence and turned red. 'Oh, I . . . er . . .'

'What are you doing out of the laboratory, Draycott?' Sam asked through his teeth. 'I thought I told you to stay put and keep an eye on that mixture?'

'I did; it cleared and I've entered it into the book.'

'Then get on with the next experiment!'

'I'll see you at lunch time in the canteen,' Annabel told Charlie. 'One o'clock as usual.' She pushed past Sam into her own laboratory, turning her head in passing to hiss, 'You big bully!' before vanishing through the door.

When she met Charlie in the canteen he was looking very uneasy and it took him some time to get to the point, but eventually he said, 'I saw Patrick yesterday.'

Blankly, Annabel nodded, resisting the temptation to say, 'So what's unusual about that?' Charlie and Patrick met almost every day, on some sports field or another, so why should Charlie look pointedly at her?

'He wanted to know if I'd upset you,' Charlie said, crimson to his very large ears. 'He said you seemed a bit dismal.'

'Oh, that's nice. Dismal, am I?' Annabel was indignant—how dare Patrick go around proclaiming her to be dismal to all and sundry? Couldn't she even feel a little heartburn without the subject being discussed from here to John o'Groat's by her whole family, friends and distant acquaintances? Why hadn't she been born an only child to parents without a relative in the world?

'Patrick thought it might be my fault,' Charlie mumbled. 'He thought maybe it was because I hadn't been around to see you lately.'

'It has nothing to do with you, don't be silly!'

Charlie looked relieved. 'Well, I didn't think it had—I mean, you more or less told me ...' he broke off, tongue-tied.

Annabel helped him out, not for the first time. 'I'm very fond of you, Charlie, but I'd like to have the chance to meet other men—and I think you should be going out with other girls, too.'

'Well, that was it,' Charlie said, swallowing like a boa constrictor having trouble with a particularly large rabbit. 'I ... I've been sort of ... seeing ...'

'Alison?' Annabel prompted kindly and he sighed, nodding.

'That's another thing—Alison was worried about dating me in case it hurt your feelings; she said I ought to get things straight with you before we went out again.'

'Things are perfectly straight, thank you, Charlie. I hope we'll always be friends, of course, but I'm very glad you're seeing Alison, she's a nice girl and I think she'll suit you splendidly.'

'Would you tell her you're glad?' he asked, brightening. 'She might not believe me. She knows we've known each other for years and I told her I'd asked you to marry me but you'd refused so obviously you wouldn't mind if I went out with her, but I don't think she understood.'

Annabel looked at him incredulously—even for Charlie, he seemed to have made a mess of things. 'Why on earth did you tell her you'd proposed? Oh, never mind. Yes, I'll speak to her, I think I'd better.' She paused. 'How are you getting on with Sam Jerrard?'

Charlie looked immediately both desperate and sulky, his lip bulging like a baby's.

'He treats me as if I was a lab assistant. I do all the work.'

'This is your project, perhaps he's trying to be tactful, leaving most of the work to you. How long is he staying here—did he say?'

'He doesn't tell me anything.' Charlie brooded, staring down at his rhubarb tart as if he suspected it was poisoned. 'I don't think he likes me,' he confided after a long pause. 'Sometimes I look up and he's staring at me as if I was a fly he was about to swat; it makes me very nervous.'

'He's a difficult man.'

'You can say that again.'

'Why not? He's difficult man,' Annabel said, getting up. 'I must go back to work. See you, Charlie, and don't worry—I'll remember to have a word with Alison.'

She didn't get a chance to see Alison for several days because the other girl was away from work, nursing a bad cold, until Thursday. It was an unbreakable rule that any member of staff who developed symptoms which were possibly infectious would stay at home. Some of the laboratory work had to be absolutely sterile; they didn't want stray germs being transmitted to anyone working on the more delicate experiments. Even in the experimental garden and greenhouses, the staff usually wore sterilised gloves and were scrupulous about equipment.

Annabel saw Sam Jerrard from time to time—it was unavoidable that they should walk past each other in corridors or in the canteen, but each time she saw him Annabel looked the other way. Sam's grey eyes were frozen wastes; he stared at her but he never said anything, and neither of them paused; they just walked on in silence.

Annabel hated him with a violence which didn't show in her cold, blank face whenever she saw him. When he asked her to come to his flat he had insulted her. She had no intention of allowing herself to be seduced, being used for his momentary entertainment while he was away from London and Denise Keiron. If he had imagined she was giving him some sort of green light, he could think again. She had always thought of herself as a modern, liberated girl. She took her job and herself seriously, she wasn't just sitting around waiting to get married—but that didn't mean that she didn't have definite standards. There were things Annabel knew she would never do—and having an affair with a man about to marry someone else was one of them.

The fact that she was in love with him made his unscrupulous, amoral, shameless behaviour all the more contemptible. How could he live like that? He was marrying Denise without loving her simply because of her money—but he obviously didn't intend to be faithful to her, either before or after marriage. Annabel felt a reluctant, angry sympathy for the other girl. No wonder Denise had wanted to check out that cottage. Sam had said he went down there to do bird-watching—but what sort of birds had he been pursuing down there?

Annabel sometimes woke up in the night with a headache and confused sense of bewilderment about the man. He had some sort of split personality—there was one Sam, who she liked and couldn't help admiring, of whom she found it hard to believe that he could ever have got engaged to a girl he didn't love just for her money—and there was the other Sam, who was ruthlessly without scruple and capable of anything.

Annabel finally managed to meet up with Alison on the Friday morning. They had coffee together in a quiet corner of the canteen, and Annabel straightened Alison out about herself and Charlie. She didn't like to be totally frank; she didn't tell Alison that she had been looking for a way of getting rid of Charlie without hurting his feelings—it made it sound as if he was an unwanted dog for whom she was trying to find a good home, and it was very clear that Alison thought Charlie was the best thing since the invention of the video. That adoring devotion was exactly what Charlie would need and Annabel smiled encouragingly as the other girl talked on and on about what a wonderful guy he was and how handsome he had looked last night when he came round to bring her some flowers. 'He said he'd missed me while I was away. My family liked him, isn't that wonderful?'

'Wonderful,' agreed Annabel.'

'I haven't met his mother yet—is she nice?'

'Has Charlie suggested taking you to see her?'

'No, not yet.' Alison looked anxious. 'Don't you think she'll like me? Is she very fond of *you*?'

'Annabel laughed. 'No, I wouldn't say that. But she's a widow and Charlie is her only child—she's possessive, Alison. I shouldn't be in any hurry to meet her, if I were you. Get to know Charlie really well first.'

Comprehension showed in Alison's face. 'Oh, dear, is it like that?'

'I'm afraid so, but don't worry about it. It's what Charlie thinks that really matters. He can't live with his mother for the rest of his life, even if she'd prefer that. Charlie needs to be rescued, in fact.'

Alison's eyes shone with steely determination at this battle cry. 'Poor Charlie! I hadn't realised.'

Annabel went back to work with a sense of achievement, smiling, but her good humour didn't last beyond lunchtime because she saw Denise Keiron crossing the car park as she was on her way out of the building. Annabel was going off to do some shopping, skipping lunch. She passed Denise without getting so much as a sideways glance. The blonde apparently never saw any member of her own sex, and, anyway, judging by the expression she was wearing when Annabel gave her one quick look as they drew level, Denise was in a temper, and in no mood to exchange polite small talk with strangers. If she hadn't been walking on delicate, expensively hand-made high heels, Annabel would have said she was stamping—that was the impression she gave.

It didn't exactly upset Annabel to guess that Sam Jerrard was about to find himself under attack. He was a grown man and could take care of himself, that Annabel knew only too well—but all the same, her money was on Denise Keiron. The blonde girl had a vicious look in her round blue eyes, and Annabel was a woman, too—she knew that the female is deadlier than the male; she'd back Denise against six men any day.

As she unlocked her car, she wished she could form an audience for whatever was going on in Sam's laboratory right now. What had he done? Why was Denise looking like an unfed tigress?

Annabel started her engine, scowling, and saw one of the lab technicians giving her a startled, apprehensive look as she almost ran him over on her way out of the car park. Annabel managed to pull an apologetic smile into her face for him, but it lapsed as she drove away towards the shopping centre. Had Sam been seeing someone else lately? If he had made a pass at her, he had probably been doing it to others. Had Denise found out that there were still other women in his life?

Blackstone had altered very little since the early nineteenth century; it was still a small country town whose streets were lined with trees, whose houses were unpretentious and solidly built. The countryside crept in wherever it got the chance; squirrels shot up and down some of the trees, annoying nesting birds, and the occasional fox came out at night to scavenge around the houses, but two years ago a new pedestrian shopping precinct had been built right in the centre where the buildings were oldest and the streets most narrow, and that was where Annabel was heading in her car.

She had no eyes today for the beauty of the morning; the blinding blue of the sky or the scented freshness of the air; the little gardens full of spring flowers, tulip and narcissi; early lilac and dark bluebells under the trees, like shifting shadows, their perfume earthy and unforgettable.

She couldn't even concentrate on her shopping

and walked around the paved precinct, staring vacantly into shop windows, hardly knowing what she was doing there. As it was a Friday, the place was crowded with hurrying women getting the weekend shopping for their families and a few old men sitting on benches in the sun reading newspapers, waiting to be collected by their wives before going home.

Annabel finally bought the new swimming costume she had come to find and on impulse bought a drop-waisted summer dress of warm orange cotton. She had to be very careful about colours; her red hair limited what she could wear, but the orange shade was perfect on her.

As she drove back into the car park at the laboratories, she quickly looked to see if Denise's gleaming Rolls Royce was still there. It was parked just opposite; she eyed it with envy and impatience. It was a beautiful toy and not for her. Denise Keiron was able to buy herself whatever she fancied—from the most expensive car to the most desirable man. Wasn't she lucky? Annabel walked across the car park, her face wry. She didn't think Denise was so lucky, in fact. Annabel had always had to work for what she wanted, but she was ready to bet that she got more of a kick out of her old, second-hand car than Denise had ever had with her streamlined dream-mobile—and Annabel wouldn't want a man money could buy. Denise was welcome to him.

Just as she got to the swing doors into the main building, Denise and Sam came out through them, and Annabel stepped out of their way quickly. She got the feeling that, if she didn't, Denise might

walk right over her. The blonde girl was talking i
a voice like the wail of an air raid warning. 'M
father isn't going to forget this in a hurry!' sh
shrieked at Sam, who was wearing a harsh
frowning expression. He put a hand unde
Denise's elbow as if to steer her towards her ca
and Denise snatched herself away, slapping hi
hand down.

Lovers' quarrel? Annabel thought cynically
Sam looked as if he had been having a bad time.

Denise was walking away when she suddenl
caught sight of Annabel—it was the very first tim
that she had ever actually *looked* at Annabel, and
for a second or two her stare was chillingly distan
and indifferent, until she skated her eyes up t
Annabel's hair and stopped in mid-step, glaring.

'Red hair!' she spat out, shuddering.

Annabel had often wished that her hair wa
some other colour, but she didn't see why Denis
should have such loathing in her voice; it seemed
rather extreme. It wasn't a social crime to have re
hair.

'My God,' Denise shrilled, her hands curling a
her sides as if she might at any moment lung
forward to pull Annabel's hair out by the roots
'It's her, isn't it? It has to be with that hair.
Denise swung round to Sam who was watching
Annabel with what seemed to be icy, accusing
eyes. 'Fire her!' Denise hissed. 'I want her out o
here today!'

CHAPTER NINE

ANNABEL couldn't believe her ears. Totally at sea, she stared at Denise wondering if this was all some sort of joke—a pretty sick joke, if it was one, she felt. But there was no amusement in the blonde girl's face; she was glaring at Annabel, her nostrils flaring and her glossy lips curled back from even, white teeth in a snarl. It was no joke.

Annabel turned to look at Sam, her eyes bewildered, questioning him—but Sam wasn't smiling, either. He looked angry; he looked mad enough to break things, and from the way he was eyeing Annabel she sensed that she was one of the things he'd like to break. She had often been angry with him herself, but the shock of meeting those savage grey eyes made the blood drain out of her body, leaving her icy cold from head to foot. Sam was looking at her as if he hated her.

'Get back to work, Miss Walsh!' he grated.

Annabel didn't argue. She turned and fled, her eyes burning with unshed tears. She was too off balance to go back into the laboratory; she dived into the cloakroom and was relieved to find it empty. She knew she was going to cry and she didn't want an audience. From babyhood, Annabel had learnt never to cry in public—her brothers only teased her if she burst into tears when she fell over or had a toy snatched away, and such a lesson is indelible. She locked herself in one of the lavatories and let the tears she had been holding back spill down her face.

She pulled herself together again pretty quickly, from sheer habit, and went out to wash her face in stingingly cold water, dry it and re-apply her make-up with hands that were now only slightly shaky. Instinct told her that the sooner she was back to normal the better, but she didn't feel she recognised the reflection in the little mirror above the wash basin. She wasn't used to such violent emotion, it had made her look very odd—her eyes were a hectic green, her lids pink and her face pale.

Even now that she was calmer, she couldn't understand what it had all been about. She was incredulous every time she remembered the fury with which Denise Keiron had screamed, 'Red hair!' at her.

Was the other girl slightly crazy? Did she have a peculiar horror of people with red hair? Perhaps she was paranoid, given to sudden whims and dislikes for no reason? She had certainly looked odd and Annabel might even have brought herself to be sorry for Denise if she hadn't been so worried. Was she really going to be fired? What if Denise insisted—would Sam give in? She had seen him giving in to Denise before; he had made Annabel hide in his cottage because he was scared of upsetting his fiancée, and when she overheard them talking Annabel remembered being surprised by the way Denise dominated the conversation. Sam hadn't struck her as a man who let his woman push him around; she had been faintly scornful of him as she listened.

Just now while Denise was screeching Sam

hadn't said anything to calm her down, had he? He hadn't tried to argue with Denise, nor had he seemed apologetic to Annabel. He had glared at her as if he hated her and snapped: 'Get back to work!'

She broke off, refusing to think about him any more, and walked out of the cloakroom to go back to her laboratory. If Sam tried to fire her when she hadn't given him any good reason to do so, she'd fight him. She wasn't being sacked because she had red hair. Just let him try! She'd take it to court and she was sure she'd have the backing of every other employee in the company. Sam was as crazy as his fiancée if he thought that he could fire someone for such a ludicrous reason.

When she opened the door of the laboratory she found all the juniors hard at work at their benches. Annabel looked at her watch, grimacing. She was twenty minutes late, a very rare occurrence for her. She sensed that she was getting pointed looks—they'd all noticed how late she was. Without a word she took down her white coat and slipped into it, washed her hands at the sink and dried them, broke open a pack of sterile gloves and put them on, then went over to begin work.

She didn't set eyes on Sam again that day. She half expected him to walk into the laboratory and all afternoon she kept looking at the door, but he did not appear. It ruined her concentration. She made several mistakes and got so angry with herself that she stopped work for fifteen minutes, went to the canteen, had a cup of tea and pulled herself together before going back to finish her task. By then, everyone else had left and she was alone in the laboratory. When she looked at her watch she realised with surprise that it was gone six and that the whole building was quiet and, probably, more or less empty.

She peeled off her gloves, washed her hands, slung her white coat among the others in the plastic laundry bin from which they would be collected by the caretaker and handed over to the private laundry which took care of all their linen, and went to the cloakroom to get her coat and brush her hair.

She met no one except the caretaker who was hanging about in the lobby, jangling his keys in a pointed way. On a Friday, he liked to get everyone out of the building dead on five-thirty so that he could lock up and retreat to his lair at the back of the building to eat his sandwiches and watch his television set. The laboratory had had an electronic burglar system installed, but Jack made his rounds every hour or so, timing them between programmes he particularly enjoyed.

'Good night, Jack. Have a nice weekend,' Annabel said and got a glum look.

'Bit late tonight, aren't you? No consideration.'

She smiled and said, 'Sorry, I forgot the time,' then went out, hearing him immediately lock the door behind her.

When she got home she was surprised to find the house dark and empty. It wasn't until she went into the kitchen that she remembered that her parents had gone to London to spend the weekend with Joe and Sandra. Patrick had been and gone— there was a note propped up against the teapot. She bent to read it. Patrick would be back late, he was taking his girlfriend to Norwich to a dance.

Annabel wished he hadn't gone out; she felt rather lonely and she needed to talk to someone. It was rare for her parents to be away overnight and when they were Annabel usually had one or other of her brothers around. She had often suspected that her parents left them as a bodyguard for her, especially during her teens. But she was no longer a teenager, she was an adult woman and perhaps it had finally dawned on the family that she did not need constant protection. She had often wished her brothers wouldn't watch over her like a pack of sheepdogs with just one lamb to protect, but contrarily she now wished one of them was here to give her a shoulder to cry on.

She hunted around for some food, feeling in no mood to cook anything elaborate, and decided to make spaghetti with a simple egg and bacon sauce. The water was boiling and she was just bending the long strands of stiff spaghetti into the water when the door bell went. Annabel frowned, looking at her watch. It might be Charlie. It was dark now, though, so when she got to the door she put the chain on and peered out warily, holding a clutch of spaghetti in one hand.

It wasn't Charlie. It was Sam in a dark green tweed jacket and green cord trousers. He looked though the gap at her with narrow-eyed hostility.

'Open up, I want to talk to you.'

'Talk,' Annabel said, making no move to take the chain off the door. 'And make it fast, because I'm in the middle of cooking my supper.' She waved the spaghetti at him in evidence.

Sam made a grab at her wrist. The spaghetti flew about and crunched under foot as Annabel shifted to break free.

'Look what you've done,' she snapped, glaring down at the hall carpet which was now littered with brittle yellow fragments. 'It will take ages to vacuum all that up and if my mother finds bits of spaghetti in the carpet when she gets back she'll murder me.'

'I may murder you first,' Sam said through his teeth. 'Your mother will have to take her place in the queue.'

Annabel wrenched away from him. 'You're not firing me because I've got red hair. You must be as crazy as your fiancée!'

'If you don't open this door I'll kick it down,' Sam promised and she got the feeling he meant it; the dark red colour in his face made it clear that he was in a dangerous temper.

'I'm not letting you in to murder me!'

'If you don't, I promise I *will* murder you,' Sam grated.

Annabel leant her whole weight on the door to close it. Sam's weight on the other side of the door forced her slowly backwards and she peered at him through the gap, getting a snarled, 'I'm losing my temper!' which convinced her that in the long run it might be safer to let him in than to have him force an entry.

Standing back she unhooked the chain, and Sam came through the door and slammed it shut. Breathing thickly, he leaned against it with his hands on his lean hips in an aggressive attitude. The spring wind had blown his black hair into disorder and she saw that he hadn't shaved for some time—his jaw had a faint stubble shadow.

'Why did you do it?' he broke out and she blinked.

'Do what?'

'Don't play the innocent with me! You know what I mean! Why did you send that letter?'

'Letter?' All day Annabel had had an increasing feeling that either she was mad and had only just realised it, or that the rest of the world was mad and she was in danger of joining them. Nobody was making sense, but whatever Sam was talking about made him so angry that his grey eyes glittered with rage.

'Don't try to fence! I've seen it. I knew it had to be you who'd sent it—who else could have known? How could you do such a thing, Annabel? There's something so sneaky and underhand about anonymous letters. I wouldn't have believed you capable of it if I hadn't seen the damned thing with my own eyes.'

Annabel had turned pale as she listened, shaken by the distaste in his face. 'I've never sent an anonymous letter in my life!' The idea that Sam could believe that she might made her feel sick.

Sam stared at her intently, his eyes penetrating. It was obvious he didn't believe her, and Annabel said angrily, 'I don't know anything about a letter—what did it say? Who was it sent to? You?'

Sam straightened and walked away down the hall towards the kitchen, which was full of steam and the bubble of boiling water. Annabel suddenly remembered the spaghetti and ran after him, but he got to the stove first and she halted, watching as he absently fed fresh spaghetti from the packet on the table into the saucepan. He did it expertly, coiling the long stalks as they softened. Only when the pan was full did he stop and look round at her.

'Denise got the letter. It was about us—whoever sent it knew that you had been at the cottage with me all night, knew that you were actually hiding in the bedroom when Denise arrived.'

Annabel sat down on a chair. Sam watched her, his mouth taut. 'It wasn't very pleasant to read,' he said and she went white, then red.

'Do you mean it was . . . obscene?'

He grimaced. 'Not exactly. It implied more than it actually said.'

'Implied what?'

He turned down the heat under the spaghetti saucepan, his back to her. 'That we were having an affair.' His voice was curt and she flinched. Sam looked round. 'And it described you in graphic detail.' His mouth curled oddly. 'That was one reason why I thought it might be you.'

She stared, bewildered.

'It made you sound like Helen of Troy,' he said with a grim sort of amusement.

'Helen of Troy? Me?' Annabel gasped and he gave her a crooked little smile, nodding.

'There was rather a lot about your red hair and green eyes, not to mention your figure.'

Her eyes opened wide; enlightment dawned. 'My hair? Is that why Denise . . .?'

'Oh, that's why,' Sam said drily. 'She had just been holding forth to me on the subject and when we walked straight into you she really blew her top. The one fact the letter-writer omitted to mention was that you worked at the laboratories, but the minute Denise set eyes on you she apparently recognised the description.' There was a sudden wicked brightness in his eyes as he ran them over Annabel. 'Would you mind if I say I thought it a little exaggerated, myself? I wouldn't have described you as quite that sexy.'

Pink, she glared at him. 'I didn't write that letter! Why on earth should I? I'm livid that you should think I had!'

'What were you going to do with this spaghetti?' he asked, glancing into the simmering pan.

'Just make spaghetti carbonara,' she told him, getting up although she still felt a little unsteady with shock.

'Mind if I share it? I'm hungry; it must be because of all the aggro I've had to put up with today.' Sam pulled the box of eggs towards him and began to break an egg into the basin Annabel had put on the table earlier. She cut the rinds off some rashers of bacon and began to fry them.

'I hope you believe me,' she said. 'I didn't send that letter, I give you my word—and I knew nothing about it, either.'

'I believe you,' Sam said. 'All the same ... I haven't told a living soul what happened at the cottage that night. So the information in that letter has to come from you, somehow. Who did you tell?'

Annabel stared at the sizzling bacon, mouth open, as it dawned on her that Sam was right.

'Draycott, was it?' asked Sam tersely, watching her. 'I know he's pretty mad at me at the moment. I've been afraid of turning my back on him in the lab in case he sticks a knife in me ...'

'Charlie would never do a thing like this! Of course it isn't Charlie.' Annabel shot him a wary look and Sam caught hold of her shoulders, his fingers digging into her.

'Come on, out with it! You've guessed, haven't you? You might as well tell me, because as sure as hell I am going to find out and when I do, the balloon is going up.'

Annabel swallowed uncertainly, eyeing him. 'Your secretary,' she said huskily. She had promised Gwen she would never tell Sam who had helped her to smuggle herself into his car, but if Gwen was going to start sending nasty anonymous letters then it was time to break her promise.

Sam stared, holding her so tightly that she winced. 'Gwen?'

She nodded and told him the rest in a breathless rush. His hands slackened and let go of her after a moment. When she stopped talking Sam stood staring at the floor, his face thunderous.

'What on earth was she up to?' he began then looked up and met Annabel's flickering eyes. She looked away, suppressing a sigh of reluctant sympathy for Gwen. She certainly wasn't telling Sam what he apparently had never guessed. Whatever Gwen had done, she deserved that much dignity.

Sam moved away to walk to the window and back in a tense prowl which made her very nervous. 'I see,' he said, almost as if to himself, and then he gave a short, impatient sigh. 'Is that bacon ready yet? The spaghetti must be cooked.'

Annabel ran to get the parmesan while he was dishing up the soft buttery loops of pasta. Sam had poured a little cream into his beaten eggs; he added the chopped, cooked bacon and then combined that mixture with the spaghetti and gently turned the whole thing once or twice before lifting some on to each of the two warmed plates Annabel had placed on the table.

'No wine?' Sam asked quizzically.

'There may be some, I hadn't intended to bother—I was just going to have a quick snack in here and then watch some TV.'

'It doesn't matter.' Sam sat down while Annabel brought out a bottle of mineral water from the fridge.

'Will this do?'

He wrinkled his nose. 'Beer would be better.'

'There's lager.' She brought it out, poured it into a glass. It was Patrick's lager and no doubt he wouldn't mind. She watched Sam generously sprinkle grated parmesan over the spaghetti, then take a forkful.

'Rather overcooked, I'm afraid,' he said. 'That's what comes of having an emotional argument while you're cooking spaghetti. Every good Italian knows you can't cook pasta and scream at the same time.'

'They always seem to.'

'That's singing, not screaming. All Italian opera should be sung while cooking and eating spaghetti; they complement each other, especially if there's a bottle of good Chianti on the table.'

Annabel twirled some spaghetti around her fork and watched it all fall off again the minute she tried to lift it to her mouth. Sam looked up, gave a grin and said, 'Try using a spoon to anchor the end of the fork and don't take so much at one time.'

She experimented and this time was successful. When she had eaten a little more she asked him hesitantly, 'What did you tell Denise?'

'The truth this time.'

'That I was at the cottage when she arrived?'

'That you'd been there all night and that you were hiding under my bed when she went into the bedroom,' he said calmly, watching the colour hit her face.

'Why on earth did you tell her *that*?'

'There seemed no point in not telling the truth by then.'

'But didn't you tell her that there was nothing to it, that we'd never had an a ...' Annabel stammered into silence and he watched her, his mouth ironic.

'I tried to—she didn't believe me.'

'But your engagement . . .'

'Is off.' He ate some more spaghetti and drank some of the lager while Annabel absorbed that information.

'If you explained . . .' she began and Sam leant over and tapped his fork on her plate.

'Eat your supper before it gets cold. It's delicious; we cook a good spaghetti. We could open a restaurant if Draycott blows up the whole building one of these days.'

'How can you just sit there, calmly eating spaghetti, when your marriage is off?' Annabel broke out. 'Denise was too upset to listen today—but when she cools down I'm sure you could make her realise the truth.'

'She knows the truth.' He gave her a mocking little smile.

Annabel's heartbeat speeded up until it deafened her. She stared at him, wide-eyed.

'What do you mean?'

Sam eyed her through his lashes. 'Everyone makes mistakes,' he said conversationally. 'Denise was one of mine. I must have been so busy that I didn't notice what I was getting myself into—she's an attractive girl, you have to give her that, a delectable looking blonde with a figure any man would describe as sexy.' His eyes teased her.

'Unlike mine, I suppose,' she muttered, highly flushed.

'Oh, yours will do,' he drawled and she was so hot she hurriedly drank some water, while Sam went on, 'Looking back, I suppose she was careful not to let me see her worst side. She was all sweetness and light whenever I was around at first, and when her father started dropping hints about marriage it didn't seem a bad idea.' He pushed away his plate and stared at hers. 'Aren't you going to eat that?'

'I'm not hungry now,' she said. 'Do you want some coffee?' She didn't want to listen to him talking about Denise Keïron any more. She didn't want to be the shoulder he cried on or to hear him describing his feelings about other women.

'Why not?' he said, watching her get up, his stare making her so self-conscious that she almost dropped the cups as she got them out of the cupboard.

'I'm nearly thirty-eight,' Sam said wryly. 'I've been too busy to think about marriage, but from time to time it did occur to me that I ought to get around to it soon before it was too late.'

'Sugar?' Annabel asked.

'No, thanks, and I take my coffee black, for future reference.'

What future? Annabel almost asked and then didn't. She kept her back to him as he went on talking in a calm, matter-of-fact voice.

'Keiron wanted me for a son-in-law and once the idea had been put into my head I decided Denise would do as well as anyone else, so I proposed one night after a party. It helped that I was slightly drunk. I think that stone cold sober I would never have got around to it. It was then that Denise dropped the veil, so to speak, and started giving me an entirely different angle on her character. She didn't say yes and she didn't say no—she's the type who enjoys playing with her conquests, like a cat with a captured mouse. Oh, she meant to say yes in the end, but once she thought I was her property she saw no point in hiding things from me.'

Annabel put the coffee on the table, frowning. 'What sort of things?'

'Her temper, for a start,' said Sam shortly. 'She is a spoilt, bad-tempered little madam, and that's partly her father's fault. He's never said no to her in her life and she doesn't see why anyone else should, either. I soon began to realise what a mistake I'd made, but I was in the middle of some very complicated business deals and I needed her father's support; I couldn't afford to offend him just at that moment. That's why I went to Brussels. Once my deals were signed, I was able to hand over the London end of the business to my deputy and, more importantly, I could afford to make it clear to Denise that she wasn't treating me as if I was a pet on a lead.'

Annabel kept her eyes lowered. 'It doesn't sound to me as if you were ever in love with her.'

'You know I wasn't,' he said with mocking intimacy and she looked up, eyes startled.

'How should I know?' she began and he laughed softly.

'Miss Butter-wouldn't-melt-in-her-mouth! You knew almost from the minute we met and you knocked me off my feet, quite literally. I was never the same again, although I couldn't work out why at first. I was irritated by the way you kept quoting Draycott at me as if he was God's second cousin. At the time I just thought how sick I was of Draycott's name; he was a thorn in my flesh before I met you. You have no idea how hard I had to fight to keep him when he kept blowing the labs up. The insurance company were on my back, I didn't need you there as well. You seemed to be obsessed with him . . .'

'I've known Charlie all my life, he's almost one of my brothers!'

'I realised that eventually, but not before he'd given me even more heart-ache. I'd never been jealous in my life before . . .'

'Jealous?' She got up, knocking over her chair, and Sam got up, too. He picked up her chair and looked at her sardonically as she backed away from him.

'Jealous,' he repeated, advancing. 'Don't pretend you didn't know.'

'Mr Jerrard,' she began and Sam laughed.

'Mr Jerrard?' he mocked. 'Why the sudden formality? Scared?'

She had backed until there was nowhere left to go and Sam was leaning over her, his hands on the wall on either side of her head, and his eyes staring down into hers, wicked lights dancing in them.

'I don't want you on the rebound,' Annabel muttered. 'You only just broke your engagement to Denise Keiron . . .'

'And I've never been so relieved in my life,' he agreed blandly.

'You looked furious when I saw you with her!'

'I was—furious with you for sending that letter, or so I thought. I was delighted with the result, I'd been wondering how to end our engagement—but I hated to think that you of all people could do such a thing; there's something about anonymous letters that makes my skin creep. I should have known it couldn't possibly be you.'

'You should! If you thought I could have done it, you can't like me much.'

Sam grimaced, frowning. 'I'm sorry, Annabel. I don't know how I could have jumped to that conclusion, but there didn't seem to be anyone else who could have had a reason to send it or the information to use in it. It was posted in Blackstone; it had to be someone at the laboratory. I thought of Draycott but it seemed more likely to be you.' He studied her angry face, sighing. 'I told myself you must have sent it to force me to break my engagement,' he admitted and she gasped.

'You thought what?'

'It seemed the only explanation. I knew I was in

love with you and I wanted to believe you loved me, too.'

She looked away, trembling. 'I don't know why you should think . . .'

He touched her mouth with one long index finger and her body melted. She leaned against the wall, afraid she might fall down without that support.

'Don't you, Annabel?' he asked softly. His finger slid across her cheek and down her throat, the slow sensuous touch of it on her skin sending shock waves along her veins.

'Stop that!' Annabel ordered, but he took no notice. He was the most unscrupulous man she had ever met—he was only too well aware of what his seductive fingers were doing to her heartbeat and his bright eyes mocked her weakness. How on earth could she distract him? Her mind was in such a state of helpless confusion that she couldn't think straight until she suddenly remembered that painting she had seen in his cottage. She looked round at him.

'Who's the woman in your painting of the cottage? One of your old flames, I suppose?' She made her tone scathing.

He looked blank. 'Woman? Painting? What are you talking about now?'

'When I was at the cottage, I saw a painting in the sitting room.'

Sam's face cleared. 'Oh, that. It wasn't anyone.'

'Don't be ridiculous—she's inside the cottage; you'd painted a reflection of her in the mirror.'

He laughed. 'I know, but I wasn't painting a real woman—when I was working on the picture I realised the cottage lacked something and on impulse I put a woman's face into the mirror; it seemed the right touch.' He looked oddly at her his face changing. 'Strangely enough, it was around then that I realised I ought to think about getting married—I suppose my sub-conscious was telling me something, pointing out that it wasn't just the cottage that lacked a woman—I did, too.'

Annabel frowned. 'I thought it might be Denise.'

'Don't be absurd—nothing like her. My dream woman was . . .' He broke off, grimacing. 'Just that—a dream. I was painting more what I felt I needed than any actual woman. I was painting happiness. I always feel happy at the cottage; it's a place where I can be free—but I'd begun to realise it wasn't quite perfect, it needed something else, someone else.' He leaned forward and began to kiss her neck before she could push him away. 'It needed you. I knew that the first time I kissed you. You'd been on my mind ever since we met at the dance, but it wasn't until I saw you at the cottage that it occurred to me that I was suffering from an old-fashioned case of love at first sight. You want to know who I painted in that mirror? It was you.'

Annabel was so breathless she could hardly speak. She turned her head away as his lips crept towards her mouth. Huskily she said, 'It looked more like hate at first sight to me!'

'No, it didn't. You knew too,' Sam contradicted, catching hold of her chin in one hand and forcing her face back towards him. 'When, Annabel? When did you know?'

Her green eyes were bright and restless as he smiled down into them.

'Tell me when you realised you were in love with me,' Sam invited.

'I didn't say I was! Don't put words into my mouth!'

'Just three,' he said. 'I.' He took her mouth gently and persuaded it to part, whispering, 'Love,' against her lips. The kiss became a slow, seductive movement Annabel found impossible to resist. 'You,' he whispered later, his hand sliding round her throat to clasp her nape and tilt her head.

Annabel could hardly breathe, let alone speak, when he lifted his head. 'Repeat the experiment at hourly intervals until there is no question of doubt about the original premise,' Sam said with husky mockery, his eyes languid between their dark lashes.

'Oh, shut up and kiss me,' she said, standing on tiptoe to meet his mouth. It was some time later that she said it: 'I love you,' not once, but several times, and Sam's arms closed around her so tightly that it seemed to Annabel something of a scientific miracle that either of them ever breathed again.

*Shay Flanagan is Gypsy,
the raven-haired beauty who inflamed passion
in the hearts of two Falconer men.*

Carole Mortimer

GYPSY

Lyon Falconer, a law unto himself, claimed Shay—when he didn't have the right. Ricky Falconer, gentle and loving married Shay—when she had no other choice.

Now her husband's death brings Shay back within Lyon's grasp. Once and for all Lyon intends to prove that Shay has always been—will always be—*his* Gypsy!